THE LOCKED ROOM

by Paul Auster

The New York Trilogy, volume 3

Sun & Moon Press

Los Angeles

Copyright © Paul Auster, 1986
Cover: Katie Messborn
Publication of this book was made possible, in part, through a
grant from the National Endowment for the Arts and through
contributions to The Contemporary Arts Educational Project, Inc.

The New American Fiction Series: 6

Library of Congress Cataloging in Publication Data

Auster, Paul, 1947–

    The Locked Room

ISBN: 0-940650-76-2
ISBN: 0-940650-77-0 (signed ed.)

FIRST EDITION
10   9   8   7   6   5   4   3   2   1

Sun & Moon Press
6363 Wilshire Boulevard, Suite 115
Los Angeles, California 90048
(213) 653-6711

1

It seems to me now that Fanshawe was always there. He is the place where everything begins for me, and without him I would hardly know who I am. We met before we could talk, babies crawling through the grass in diapers, and by the time we were seven we had pricked our fingers with pins and made ourselves blood brothers for life. Whenever I think of my childhood now, I see Fanshawe. He was the one who was with me, the one who shared my thoughts, the one I saw whenever I looked up from myself.

But that was a long time ago. We grew up, went off to different places, drifted apart. None of that is very strange, I think. Our lives carry us along in ways we cannot control, and almost nothing stays with us. It dies when we do, and death is something that happens to us every day.

Seven years ago this November, I received a letter from a woman named Sophie Fanshawe. "You don't know me," the letter began, "and I apologize for writing to you like this out of the blue. But things have happened, and under the circumstances I don't have much choice." It turned out that she was Fanshawe's wife. She knew that I had grown up with her husband, and she also knew that I lived in New York, since she had read many of the articles I had published in magazines.

The explanation came in the second paragraph, very bluntly, without any preamble. Fanshawe had disappeared, she wrote, and it was more than six months since she had last seen him. Not a word in all that time, not the slightest clue as to where he might be. The police had found no trace of him, and the private detective she hired to look for him had come up empty-handed. Nothing was sure, but the facts seemed to speak for themselves: Fanshawe was probably dead; it was pointless to think he would be coming back. In the light of all this, there was something important she needed to discuss with me, and she wondered if I would agree to see her.

This letter caused a series of little shocks in me. There was too much information to absorb all at once; too many forces were pulling me in different directions. Out of nowhere, Fanshawe had suddenly reappeared in my life. But no sooner was his name mentioned than he had vanished again. He was married, he had been living in New York—and I knew nothing about him anymore. Selfishly, I felt hurt that he had not bothered to get in touch with me. A phone call, a post card, a drink to catch up on old times—it would not have been difficult to arrange. But the fault was equally my own. I knew where Fanshawe's mother lived, and if I had wanted to find him, I could easily have asked her. The fact was that I had let go of Fanshawe. His life had stopped the moment we went our separate ways, and he belonged to the past for me now, not to the present. He was a ghost I carried around inside me, a prehistoric figment, a thing that was no longer real. I tried to remember the last time I had seen him, but nothing was clear. My mind wandered for several minutes and then stopped short, fixing on the day his father died. We were in high school then and could not have been more than seventeen years old.

I called Sophie Fanshawe and told her I would be glad to see her whenever it was convenient. We decided on the following day, and she sounded grateful, even though I explained to her that I had not heard from Fanshawe and had no idea where he was.

She lived in a red-brick tenement in Chelsea, an old walk-up building with gloomy stairwells and peeling paint on the walls. I climbed the five flights to her floor, accompanied by the sounds of radios and squabbles and flushing toilets that came from the apartments on the way up, paused to catch my breath, and then knocked. An eye looked through the peephole in the door, there was a clatter of bolts being turned, and then Sophie Fanshawe was standing before me, holding a small baby in her left arm. As she smiled at me and invited me in, the baby tugged at her long brown hair. She ducked away gently from the attack, took hold of the child with her two hands, and turned him face front towards me. This was Ben, she said, Fanshawe's son, and he had been born just three-and-a-half months ago. I pretended to admire the baby, who was waving his arms and drooling whitish spittle down his chin, but I was more interested in his mother. Fanshawe had been lucky. The woman was beautiful, with dark, intelligent eyes, almost fierce in their steadiness. Thin, not more than average height, and with something slow in her manner, a thing that made her both sensual and watchful, as though she looked out on the world from the heart of a deep inner vigilance. No man would have left this woman of his own free will—especially not when she was about to have his child. That much was certain to me. Even before I stepped into the apartment, I knew that Fanshawe had to be dead.

It was a small railroad flat with four rooms, sparsely furnished, with one room set aside for books and a work table, another that served as the living room, and the last two for sleeping. The place was well-ordered, shabby in its details, but on the whole not uncomfortable. If nothing else, it proved that Fanshawe had not spent his time making money. But I was not one to look down my nose at shabbiness. My own apartment was even more cramped and dark than this one, and I knew what it was to struggle each month to come up with the rent.

Sophie Fanshawe gave me a chair to sit in, made me a cup of coffee, and then sat down on the tattered blue sofa. With the baby on her lap, she told me the story of Fanshawe's disappearance.

They had met in New York three years ago. Within a month they had moved in together, and less than a year after that they were married. Fanshawe was not an easy man to live with, she said, but she loved him, and there had never been anything in his behavior to suggest that he did not love her. They had been happy together; he had been looking forward to the birth of the baby; there was no bad blood between them. One day in April he told her that he was going to New Jersey for the afternoon to see his mother, and then he did not come back. When Sophie called her mother-in-law late that night, she learned that Fanshawe had never made the visit. Nothing like this had ever happened before, but Sophie decided to wait it out. She didn't want to be one of those wives who panicked whenever her husband failed to show up, and she knew that Fanshawe needed more breathing room than most men. She even decided not to ask any questions when he returned home. But then a week went by, and then another week, and at last she went to the police. As she expected, they were not overly concerned about her problem. Unless there was evidence of a crime, there was little they could do. Husbands, after all, deserted their wives every day, and most of them did not want to be found. The police made a few routine inquiries, came up with nothing, and then suggested that she hire a private detective. With the help of her mother-in-law, who offered to pay the costs, she engaged the services of a man named Quinn. Quinn worked doggedly on the case for five or six weeks, but in the end he begged off, not wanting to take any more of their money. He told Sophie that Fanshawe was most likely still in the country, but whether alive or dead he could not say. Quinn was no charlatan. Sophie found him sympathetic, a man who genuinely wanted to help, and when he came to her that last day she realized it was impossible to argue against his verdict. There was nothing to be done. If Fanshawe had decided to leave her, he would not have stolen off without a word. It was not like him to shy away from the truth, to back down from unpleasant confrontations. His disappearance could therefore mean only one thing: that some terrible harm had come to him.

Still, Sophie went on hoping that something would turn up. She had read about cases of amnesia, and for a while this took hold of her as a desperate possibility: the thought of Fanshawe staggering around somewhere not knowing who he was, robbed of his life but nevertheless alive, perhaps on the verge of returning to himself at any moment. More weeks passed, and then the end of her pregnancy began to approach. The baby was due in less than a month—which meant that it could come at any time—and little by little the unborn child began to take up all her thoughts, as though there was no more room inside her for Fanshawe. These were the words she used to describe the feeling—no more room inside her—and then she went on to say that this probably meant that in spite of everything she was angry at Fanshawe, angry at him for having abandoned her, even though it wasn't his fault. This statement struck me as brutally honest. I had never heard anyone talk about personal feelings like that—so unsparingly, with such disregard for conventional pieties—and as I write this now, I realize that even on that first day I had slipped through a hole in the earth, that I was falling into a place where I had never been before.

One morning, Sophie continued, she woke up after a difficult night and understood that Fanshawe would not be coming back. It was a sudden, absolute truth, never again to be questioned. She cried then, and went on crying for a week, mourning Fanshawe as though he were dead. When the tears stopped, however, she found herself without regrets. Fanshawe had been given to her for a number of years, she decided, and that was all. Now there was the child to think about, and nothing else really mattered. She knew this sounded rather pompous—but the fact was that she continued to live with this sense of things, and it continued to make life possible for her.

I asked her a series of questions, and she answered each one calmly, deliberately, as though making an effort not to color the responses with her own feelings. How they had lived, for example, and what work Fanshawe had done, and what had happened to him in the years since I had last seen him. The baby started fussing on the sofa, and without any pause in the conversation, Sophie opened her blouse and nursed him, first on one breast and then on the other.

She could not be sure of anything prior to her first meeting with Fanshawe, she said. She knew that he had dropped out of college after two years, had managed to get a deferment from the army, and wound up working on a ship of some sort for a while. An oil tanker, she thought, or perhaps a freighter. After that, he had lived in France for several years—first in Paris, then as the caretaker of a farmhouse in the South. But all this was quite dim to her, since Fanshawe had never talked much about the past. At the time they met, he had not been back in America more than eight or ten months. They literally bumped into each other—the two of them standing by the door of a Manhattan bookshop one wet Saturday afternoon, looking through the window and waiting for the rain to stop. That was the beginning, and from that day until the day Fanshawe disappeared, they had been together nearly all the time.

Fanshawe had never had any regular work, she said, nothing that could be called a real job. Money didn't mean much to him, and he tried to think about it as little as possible. In the years before he met Sophie, he had done all kinds of things—the stint in the merchant marine, working in a warehouse, tutoring, ghost writing, waiting on tables, painting apartments, hauling furniture for a moving company—but each job was temporary, and once he had earned enough to keep himself going for a few months, he would quit. When he and Sophie began living together, Fanshawe did not work at all. She had a job teaching music in a private school, and her salary could support them both. They had to be careful, of course, but there was always food on the table, and neither of them had any complaints.

I did not interrupt. It seemed clear to me that this catalogue was only a beginning, details to be disposed of before turning to the business at hand. Whatever Fanshawe had done with his life, it had little connection with this list of odd jobs. I knew this immediately, in advance of anything that was said. We were not talking about just anyone, after all. This was Fanshawe, and the past was not so remote that I could not remember who he was.

Sophie smiled when she saw that I was ahead of her, that I knew what was coming. I think she had expected me to know, and this merely confirmed that expectation, erasing any doubts she might have had about asking me to come. I knew without having to be told, and that gave me the right to be there, to be listening to what she had to say.

"He went on with his writing," I said. "He became a writer, didn't he?"

Sophie nodded. That was exactly it. Or part of it, in any case. What puzzled me was why I had never heard of him. If Fanshawe was a writer, then surely I would have run across his name somewhere. It was my business to know about these things, and it seemed unlikely that Fanshawe, of all people, would have escaped my attention. I wondered if he had been unable to find a publisher for his work. It was the only question that seemed logical.

No, Sophie said, it was more complicated than that. He had never tried to publish. At first, when he was very young, he was too timid to send anything out, feeling that his work was not good enough. But even later, when his confidence had grown, he discovered that he preferred to stay in hiding. It would distract him to start looking for a publisher, he told her, and when it came right down to it, he would much rather spend his time on the work itself. Sophie was upset by this indifference, but whenever she pressed him about it, he would answer with a shrug: there's no rush, sooner or later he would get around to it.

Once or twice, she actually thought of taking matters into her own hands and smuggling a manuscript out to a publisher, but she never went through with it. There were rules in a marriage that couldn't be broken, and no matter how wrong-headed his attitude was, she had little choice but to go along with him. There was a great quantity of work, she said, and it maddened her to think of it just sitting there in the closet, but Fanshawe deserved her loyalty, and she did her best to say nothing.

One day, about three or four months before he disappeared, Fanshawe came to her with a compromise gesture. He gave her his word that he would do something about it within a year, and to prove that he meant it, he told her that if for any reason he failed to keep up his end of the bargain, she was to take all his manuscripts to me and put them in my hands. I was the guardian of his work, he said, and it was up to me to decide what should happen to it. If I thought it was worth publishing, he would give in to my judgment. Furthermore, he said, if anything should happen to him in the meantime, she was to give me the manuscripts at once and allow me to make all the arrangements, with the understanding that I would receive twenty-five percent of any money the work happened to earn. If I thought his writings were not worth publishing, however, then I should return the manuscripts to Sophie, and she was to destroy them, right down to the last page.

These pronouncements startled her, Sophie said, and she almost laughed at Fanshawe for being so solemn about it. The whole scene was out of character for him, and she wondered if it didn't have something to do with the fact that she had just become pregnant. Perhaps the idea of fatherhood had sobered him into a new sense of responsibility; perhaps he was so determined to prove his good intentions that he had overstated the case. Whatever the reason, she found herself glad that he had changed his mind. As her pregnancy advanced, she even began to have secret dreams of Fanshawe's success, hoping that she would be able to quit her job and raise the child without any financial pressure. Everything had gone wrong, of course, and Fanshawe's work was soon forgotten, lost in the turmoil that followed his disappearance. Later, when the dust began to settle, she had resisted carrying out his instructions—for fear that it would jinx any chance she had of seeing him again. But eventually she gave in, knowing that Fanshawe's word had to be respected. That was why she had written to me. That was why I was sitting with her now.

For my part, I didn't know how to react. The proposition had caught me off guard, and for a minute or two I just sat there, wrestling with the enormous thing that had been thrust at me. As far as I could tell, there was no earthly reason for Fanshawe to have chosen me for this job. I had not seen him in more than ten years, and I was almost surprised to learn that he still remembered who I was. How could I be expected to take on such a responsibility—to stand in judgment of a man and say whether his life had been worth living? Sophie tried to explain. Fanshawe had not been in touch, she said, but he had often talked to her about me, and each time my name had been mentioned, I was described as his best friend in the world—the one true friend he had ever had. He had also managed to keep up with my work, always buying the magazines in which my articles appeared, and sometimes even reading the pieces aloud to her. He admired what I did, Sophie said; he was proud of me, and he felt that I had it in me to do something great.

All this praise embarrassed me. There was so much intensity in Sophie's voice, I somehow felt that Fanshawe was speaking through her, telling me these things with his own lips. I admit that I was flattered, and no doubt that was a natural feeling under the circumstances. I was having a hard time of it just then, and the fact was that I did not share this high opinion of myself. I had written a great many articles, it was true, but I did not see that as a cause for celebration, nor was I particularly proud of it. As far as I was concerned, it was just a little short of hack work. I had begun with great hopes, thinking that I would become a novelist, thinking that I would eventually be able to write something that would touch people and make a difference in their lives. But time went on, and little by little I realized that this was not going to happen. I did not have such a book inside me, and at a certain point I told myself to give up my dreams. It was simpler to go on writing articles in any case. By working hard, by moving steadily from one piece to the next, I could more or less earn a living—and, for whatever it was worth, I had the pleasure of seeing my name in print almost constantly. I understood that things could have been far more dismal than they were. I was not quite thirty, and already I had something of a reputation. I had begun with reviews of poetry and novels, and now I could write about nearly anything and do a creditable job. Movies, plays, art shows, concerts, books, even baseball games—they had only to ask me, and I would do it. The world saw me as a bright young fellow, a new critic on the rise, but inside myself I felt old, already used up. What I had done so far amounted to a mere fraction of nothing at all. It was so much dust, and the slightest wind would blow it away.

Fanshawe's praise, therefore, left me with mixed feelings. On the one hand, I knew that he was wrong. On the other hand (and this is where it gets murky), I wanted to believe that he was right. I thought: is it possible that I've been too hard on myself? And once I began to think that, I was lost. But who wouldn't jump at the chance to redeem himself— what man is strong enough to reject the possibility of hope? The thought flickered through me that I could one day be resurrected in my own eyes, and I felt a sudden burst of friendship for Fanshawe across the years, across all the silence of the years that had kept us apart.

That was how it happened. I succumbed to the flattery of a man who wasn't there, and in that moment of weakness I said yes. I'll be glad to read the work, I said, and do whatever I can to help. Sophie smiled at this—whether from happiness or disappointment I could never tell—and then stood up from the sofa and carried the baby into the next room. She stopped in front of a tall oak cupboard, unlatched the door, and let it swing open on its hinges. There you are, she said. There were boxes and binders and folders and notebooks cramming the shelves—more things than I would have thought possible. I remember laughing with embarrassment and making some feeble joke. Then, all business, we discussed the best way for me to carry the

manuscripts out of the apartment, eventually deciding on
two large suitcases. It took the better part of an hour, but
in the end we managed to squeeze everything in. Clearly, I
said, it was going to take me some time to sift through all the
material. Sophie told me not to worry, and then she
apologized for burdening me with such a job. I said that I
understood, that there was no way she could have refused
to carry out Fanshawe's request. It was all very dramatic,
and at the same time gruesome, almost comical. The
beautiful Sophie delicately put the baby down on the floor,
gave me a great hug of thanks, and then kissed me on the
cheek. For a moment I thought she was going to cry, but the
moment passed and there were no tears. Then I hauled the
two suitcases slowly down the stairs and onto the street.
Together, they were as heavy as a man.

2

The truth is far less simple than I would like it to be. That I loved Fanshawe, that he was my closest friend, that I knew him better than anyone else—these are facts, and nothing I say can ever diminish them. But that is only a beginning, and in my struggle to remember things as they really were, I see now that I also held back from Fanshawe, that a part of me always resisted him. Especially as we grew older, I do not think I was ever entirely comfortable in his presence. If envy is too strong a word for what I am trying to say, then I would call it a suspicion, a secret feeling that Fanshawe was somehow better than I was. All this was unknown to me at the time, and there was never anything specific that I could point to. Yet the feeling lingered that there was more innate goodness in him than in others, that some unquenchable fire was keeping him alive, that he was more truly himself than I could ever hope to be.

Early on, his influence was already quite pronounced. This extended even to very small things. If Fanshawe wore his belt buckle on the side of his pants, then I would move my belt into the same position. If Fanshawe came to the playground wearing black sneakers, then I would ask for black sneakers the next time my mother took me to the shoe store. If Fanshawe brought a copy of *Robinson Crusoe* with him to school, then I would begin reading *Robinson Crusoe* that same evening at home. I was not the only one who behaved like this, but I was perhaps the most devoted, the one who gave in most willingly to the power he held over us. Fanshawe himself was not aware of that power, and no doubt that was the reason he continued to hold it. He was indifferent to the attention he received, calmly going about his business, never using his influence to manipulate others. He did not play the pranks the rest of us did; he did not make mischief; he did not get into trouble with the teachers. But no one held this against him. Fanshawe stood apart from us, and yet he was the one who held us together, the one we approached to arbitrate our disputes, the one we could count on to be fair and to cut through our petty quarrels. There was something so attractive about him that you always wanted him beside you, as if you could live within his sphere and be touched by what he was. He was there for you, and yet at the same time he was inaccessible. You felt there was a secret core in him that could never be penetrated, a mysterious center of hiddenness. To imitate him was somehow to participate in that mystery, but it was also to understand that you could never really know him.

I am talking about our very early childhood—as far back as five, six, seven years old. Much of it is buried now, and

I know that even memories can be false. Still, I don't think I would be wrong in saying that I have kept the aura of those days inside me, and to the extent that I can feel what I felt then, I doubt those feelings can lie. Whatever it was that Fanshawe eventually became, my sense is that it started for him back then. He formed himself very quickly, was already a sharply defined presence by the time we started school. Fanshawe was visible, whereas the rest of us were creatures without shape, in the throes of constant tumult, floundering blindly from one moment to the next. I don't mean to say that he grew up fast—he never seemed older than he was—but that he was already himself before he grew up. For one reason or another, he never became subject to the same upheavals as the rest of us. His dramas were of a different order—more internal, no doubt more brutal—but with none of the abrupt changes that seemed to punctuate everyone else's life.

One incident is particularly vivid to me. It concerns a birthday party that Fanshawe and I were invited to in the first or second grade, which means that it falls at the very beginning of the period I am able to talk about with any precision. It was a Saturday afternoon in spring, and we walked to the party with another boy, a friend of ours named Dennis Walden. Dennis had a much harder life than either of us did: an alcoholic mother, an overworked father, innumerable brothers and sisters. I had been to his house two or three times—a great, dark ruin of a place—

and I can remember being frightened by his mother, who made me think of a fairy tale witch. She would spend the whole day behind the closed door of her room, always in her bathrobe, her pale face a nightmare of wrinkles, poking her head out every now and then to scream something at the children. On the day of the party, Fanshawe and I had been duly equipped with presents to give the birthday boy, all wrapped in colorful paper and tied with ribbons. Dennis, however, had nothing, and he felt bad about it. I can remember trying to console him with some empty phrase or other: it didn't matter, no one really cared, in all the confusion it wouldn't be noticed. But Dennis did care, and that was what Fanshawe immediately understood. Without any explanation, he turned to Dennis and handed him his present. Here, he said, take this one—I'll tell them I left mine at home. My first reaction was to think that Dennis would resent the gesture, that he would feel insulted by Fanshawe's pity. But I was wrong. He hesitated for a moment, trying to absorb this sudden change of fortune, and then nodded his head, as if acknowledging the wisdom of what Fanshawe had done. It was not an act of charity so much as an act of justice, and for that reason Dennis was able to accept it without humiliating himself. The one thing had been turned into the other. It was a piece of magic, a combination of off-handedness and total conviction, and I doubt that anyone but Fanshawe could have pulled it off.

After the party, I went back with Fanshawe to his house.

His mother was there, sitting in the kitchen, and she asked us about the party and whether the birthday boy had liked the present she had bought for him. Before Fanshawe had a chance to say anything, I blurted out the story of what he had done. I had no intention of getting him into trouble, but it was impossible for me to keep it to myself. Fanshawe's gesture had opened up a whole new world for me: the way someone could enter the feelings of another and take them on so completely that his own were no longer important. It was the first truly moral act I had witnessed, and nothing else seemed worth talking about. Fanshawe's mother was not so enthusiastic, however. Yes, she said, that was a kind and generous thing to do, but it was also wrong. The present had cost her money, and by giving it away Fanshawe had in some sense stolen that money from her. On top of that, Fanshawe had acted impolitely by showing up without a present—which reflected badly on her, since she was the one responsible for his actions. Fanshawe listened carefully to his mother and did not say a word. After she was finished, he still did not speak, and she asked him if he understood. Yes, he said, he understood. It probably would have ended there, but then, after a short pause, Fanshawe went on to say that he still thought he was right. It didn't matter to him how she felt: he would do the same thing again the next time. A scene followed this little exchange. Mrs. Fanshawe became angry at his imperti- nence, but Fanshawe stuck to his guns, refusing to budge under the barrage of her reprimands. Eventually, he was ordered to his room and I was told to leave the house. I was appalled by his mother's unfairness, but when I tried to speak up in his defense, Fanshawe waved me off. Rather than protest anymore, he took his punishment silently and disappeared into his room.

The whole episode was pure Fanshawe: the spontaneous act of goodness, the unswerving belief in what he had done, and the mute, almost passive giving in to its consequences. No matter how remarkable his behavior was, you always felt that he was detached from it. More than anything else, it was this quality that sometimes scared me away from him. I would get so close to Fanshawe, would admire him so intensely, would want so desperately to measure up to him—and then, suddenly, a moment would come when I realized that he was alien to me, that the way he lived inside himself could never correspond to the way I needed to live. I wanted too much of things, I had too many desires, I lived too fully in the grip of the immediate ever to attain such indifference. It mattered to me that I do well, that I impress people with the empty signs of my ambition: good grades, varsity letters, awards for whatever it was they were judging us on that week. Fanshawe remained aloof from all that, quietly standing in his corner, paying no attention. If he did well, it was always in spite of himself, with no struggle, no effort, no stake in the thing he had done. This posture could be unnerving, and it took me a long time to learn that what was good for Fanshawe was not necessarily good for me.

I do not want to exaggerate, however. If Fanshawe and I eventually had our differences, what I remember most about our childhood is the passion of our friendship. We lived next door to each other, and our fenceless backyards merged into an unbroken stretch of lawn, gravel, and dirt, as though we belonged to the same household. Our mothers were close friends, our fathers were tennis partners, neither one of us had a brother: ideal conditions therefore, with nothing to stand between us. We were born less than a week apart and spent our babyhoods in the backyard together, exploring the grass on all fours, tearing apart the flowers, standing up and taking our first steps on the same day. (There are photographs to document this.) Later, we learned baseball and football in the backyard together. We built our forts, played our games, invented our worlds in the backyard, and still later, there were our rambles through the town, the long afternoons on our bicycles, the endless conversations. It would be impossible, I think, for me to know anyone as well as I knew Fanshawe then. My mother recalls that we were so attached to each other that once, when we were six, we asked her if it was possible for men to get married. We wanted to live together when we grew up, and who else but married people did that? Fanshawe was going to be an astronomer, and I was going to be a vet. We were thinking of a big house in the country—a place where the sky would be dark enough at night to see all the stars and where there would be no shortage of animals to take care of.

In retrospect, I find it natural that Fanshawe should have become a writer. The severity of his inwardness almost seemed to demand it. Even in grammar school he was composing little stories, and I doubt there was ever a time after the age of ten or eleven when he did not think of himself as a writer. In the beginning, of course, it didn't seem to mean much. Poe and Stevenson were his models, and what came out of it was the usual boyish claptrap. "One night, in the year of our Lord seventeen hundred and fifty-one, I was walking through a murderous blizzard toward the house of my ancestors, when I chanced upon a spectre-like figure in the snow." That kind of thing, filled with overblown phrases and extravagant turns of plot. In the sixth grade, I remember, Fanshawe wrote a short detective novel of about fifty pages, which the teacher let him read to the class in ten-minute installments each day at the end of school. We were all proud of Fanshawe and surprised by the dramatic way he read, acting out the parts of each of the characters. The story escapes me now, but I recall that it was infinitely complex, with the outcome hinging on something like the confused identities of two sets of twins.

Fanshawe was not a bookish child, however. He was too good at games for that, too central a figure among us to retreat into himself. All through those early years, one had the impression there was nothing he did not do well, nothing he did not do better than everyone else. He was the best baseball player, the best student, the best looking of all the boys. Any one of these things would have been enough to give him special status—but together they made him seem heroic, a child who had been touched by the gods. Extraordinary as he was, however, he remained one of us. Fanshawe was not a boy-genius or a prodigy; he did not have any miraculous gift that would have set him apart from the children his own age. He was a perfectly normal child—but more so, if that is possible, more in harmony with himself, more ideally a normal child than any of the rest of us.

At heart, the Fanshawe I knew was not a bold person. Nevertheless, there were times when he shocked me by his willingness to jump into dangerous situations. Behind all the surface composure, there seemed to be a great darkness: an urge to test himself, to take risks, to haunt the edges of things. As a boy, he had a passion for playing around construction sites, clambering up ladders and scaffolds, balancing on planks over an abyss of machinery, sandbags, and mud. I would hover in the background as Fanshawe performed these stunts, silently imploring him to stop, but never saying anything—wanting to go, but afraid to lest he should fall. As time went on, these impulses became more articulate. Fanshawe would talk to me about

the importance of "tasting life." Making things hard for
yourself, he said, searching out the unknown—this was
what he wanted, and more and more as he got older. Once,
when we were about fifteen, he persuaded me to spend the
weekend with him in New York—roaming the streets,
sleeping on a bench in the old Penn Station, talking to
bums, seeing how long we could last without eating. I
remember getting drunk at seven o'clock on Sunday morning in Central Park and puking all over the grass. For
Fanshawe this was essential business—another step toward
proving oneself—but for me it was only sordid, a miserable
lapse into something I was not. Still, I continued to go along
with him, a befuddled witness, sharing in the quest but not
quite part of it, an adolescent Sancho astride my donkey,
watching my friend do battle with himself.

A month or two after our weekend on the bum, Fanshawe
took me to a brothel in New York (a friend of his arranged
the visit), and it was there that we lost our virginity. I
remember a small brownstone apartment on the Upper
West Side near the river—a kitchenette and one dark
bedroom with a flimsy curtain hanging between them.
There were two black women in the place, one fat and old,
the other young and pretty. Since neither one of us wanted
the older woman, we had to decide who would go first. If
memory serves, we actually went into the hall and flipped a
coin. Fanshawe won, of course, and two minutes later I
found myself sitting in the little kitchen with the fat madam.

She called me sugar, reminding me every so often that she
was still available, in case I had a change of heart. I was too
nervous to do anything but shake my head, and then I just
sat there, listening to Fanshawe's intense and rapid breathing on the other side of the curtain. I could only think about
one thing: that my dick was about to go into the same place
that Fanshawe's was now. Then it was my turn, and to this
day I have no idea what the girl's name was. She was the
first naked woman I had seen in the flesh, and she was so
casual and friendly about her nakedness that things might
have gone well for me if I hadn't been distracted by
Fanshawe's shoes—visible in the gap between the curtain
and the floor, shining in the light of the kitchen, as if
detached from his body. The girl was sweet and did her best
to help me, but it was a long struggle, and even at the end
I felt no real pleasure. Afterward, when Fanshawe and I
walked out into the twilight, I didn't have much to say for
myself. Fanshawe, however, seemed rather content, as if
the experience had somehow confirmed his theory about
tasting life. I realized then that Fanshawe was much
hungrier than I could ever be.

We led a sheltered life out there in the suburbs. New
York was only twenty miles away, but it could have been
China for all it had to do with our little world of lawns and
wooden houses. By the time he was thirteen or fourteen,
Fanshawe became a kind of internal exile, going through
the motions of dutiful behavior, but cut off from his

surroundings, contemptuous of the life he was forced to live. He did not make himself difficult or outwardly rebellious, he simply withdrew. After commanding so much attention as a child, always standing at the exact center of things, Fanshawe almost disappeared by the time we reached high school, shunning the spotlight for a stubborn marginality. I knew that he was writing seriously by then (although by the age of sixteen he had stopped showing his work to anyone), but I take that more as a symptom than as a cause. In our sophomore year, for example, Fanshawe was the only member of our class to make the varsity baseball team. He played extremely well for several weeks, and then, for no apparent reason, quit the team. I remember listening to him describe the incident to me the day after it happened: walking into the coach's office after practice and turning in his uniform. The coach had just taken his shower, and when Fanshawe entered the room he was standing by his desk stark naked, a cigar in his mouth and his baseball cap on his head. Fanshawe took pleasure in the description, dwelling on the absurdity of the scene, embellishing it with details about the coach's squat, pudgy body, the light in the room, the puddle of water on the gray concrete floor—but that was all it was, a description, a string of words divorced from anything that might have concerned Fanshawe himself. I was disappointed that he had quit, but Fanshawe never really explained what he had done, except to say that he found baseball boring.

As with many gifted people, a moment came when Fanshawe was no longer satisfied with doing what came easily to him. Having mastered all that was demanded of him at an early age, it was probably natural that he should begin to look for challenges elsewhere. Given the limitations of his life as a high school student in a small town, the fact that he found that elsewhere inside himself is neither surprising nor unusual. But there was more to it than that, I believe. Things happened around that time in Fanshawe's family that no doubt made a difference, and it would be wrong not to mention them. Whether they made an essential difference is another story, but I tend to think that everything counts. In the end, each life is no more than the sum of contingent facts, a chronicle of chance intersections, of flukes, of random events that divulge nothing but their own lack of purpose.

When Fanshawe was sixteen, it was discovered that his father had cancer. For a year and a half he watched his father die, and during that time the family slowly unravelled. Fanshawe's mother was perhaps hardest hit. Stoically keeping up appearances, attending to the business of medical consultations, financial arrangements, and trying to maintain the household, she swung fitfully between great optimism over the chances of recovery and a kind of paralytic despair. According to Fanshawe, she was never able to accept the one inevitable fact that kept staring her in the face. She knew what was going to happen, but she did not have the strength to admit that she knew, and as time went on she began to live as though she were holding her breath. Her behavior became more and more eccentric: all-night binges of manic house cleaning, a fear of being in the house alone (combined with sudden, unexplained absences from the house), and a whole range of imagined ailments (allergies, high blood pressure, dizzy spells). Toward the end, she started taking an interest in various crackpot theories—astrology, psychic phenomena, vague spiritualist notions about the soul—until it became impossible to talk to her without being worn down to silence as she lectured on the corruption of the human body.

Relations between Fanshawe and his mother became tense. She clung to him for support, acting as though the family's pain belonged only to her. Fanshawe had to be the solid one in the house; not only did he have to take care of himself, he had to assume responsibility for his sister, who was just twelve at the time. But this brought with it another set of problems—for Ellen was a troubled, unstable child, and in the parental void that ensued from the illness she began to look to Fanshawe for everything. He became her father, her mother, her bastion of wisdom and comfort. Fanshawe understood how unhealthy her dependence on him was, but there was little he could do about it short of hurting her in some irreparable way. I remember how my own mother would talk about "poor Jane" (Mrs. Fanshawe) and how terrible the whole thing was for the "baby." But I knew that in some sense it was Fanshawe who suffered the most. It was just that he never got a chance to show it.

As for Fanshawe's father, there is little I can say with any certainty. He was a cipher to me, a silent man of abstracted benevolence, and I never got to know him well. Whereas my father tended to be around a lot, especially on the week-ends, Fanshawe's father was rarely to be seen. He was a lawyer of some prominence, and at one time he had had political ambitions—but these had ended in a series of disappointments. He usually worked until late, pulling into the driveway at eight or nine o'clock, and often spent Saturday and part of Sunday at his office. I doubt that he ever knew quite what to make of his son, for he seemed to be a man with little feeling for children, someone who had lost all memory of having been a child himself. Mr. Fanshawe was so thoroughly adult, so completely immersed in serious, grown-up matters, that I imagine it was hard for him not to think of us as creatures from another world.

He was not yet fifty when he died. For the last six months of his life, after the doctors had given up hope of saving him, he lay in the spare bedroom of the Fanshawe house, watching the yard through the window, reading an occa-sional book, taking his pain-killers, dozing. Fanshawe spent most of his free time with him then, and though I can only speculate on what happened, I assume that things changed between them. At the very least, I know how hard he worked at it, often staying home from school to be with him, trying to make himself indispensable, nursing him with unflinching attentiveness. It was a grim thing for Fanshawe to go through, too much for him perhaps, and though he seemed to take it well, summoning up the bravery that is possible only in the very young, I sometimes wonder if he ever managed to get over it.

There is only one more thing I want to mention here. At the end of this period—the very end, when no one expected Fanshawe's father to last more than a few days—Fanshawe and I went for a drive after school. It was February, and a few minutes after we started, a light snow began to fall. We drove aimlessly, looping through some of the neighboring towns, paying little attention to where we were. Ten or fifteen miles from home, we came upon a cemetery; the gate happened to be open, and for no particular reason we decided to drive in. After a while, we stopped the car and began to wander around on foot. We read the inscriptions on the stones, speculated on what each of those lives might have been, fell silent, walked some more, talked, fell silent again. By now the snow was coming down heavily, and the ground was turning white. Somewhere in the middle of the cemetery there was a freshly dug grave, and Fanshawe and I stopped at the edge and looked down into it. I can remember how quiet it was, how far away the world seemed to be from us. For a long time neither one of us spoke, and then Fanshawe said that he wanted to see what it was like at the bottom. I gave him my hand and held on tightly as he lowered himself into the grave. When his feet touched the ground he looked back up at me with a half-smile, and then lay down on his back, as though pretending to be dead. It is still completely vivid to me: looking down at Fanshawe as he looked up at the sky, his eyes blinking furiously as the snow fell onto his face.

By some obscure train of thought, it made me think back to when we were very small—no more than four or five years old. Fanshawe's parents had bought some new appliance, a television perhaps, and for several months Fanshawe kept the cardboard box in his room. He had always been generous in sharing his toys, but this box was off limits to me, and he never let me go in it. It was his secret place, he told me, and when he sat inside and closed it up around him, he could go wherever he wanted to go, could be wherever he wanted to be. But if another person ever entered his box, then its magic would be lost for good. I believed this story and did not press him for a turn, although it nearly broke my heart. We would be playing in his room, quietly setting up soldiers or drawing pictures, and then, out of the blue, Fanshawe would announce that he was going into his box. I would try to go on with what I had been doing, but it was never any use. Nothing interested me so much as what was happening to Fanshawe inside the box, and I would spend those minutes desperately trying to imagine the adventures he was having. But I never learned what they were, since it was also against the rules for Fanshawe to talk about them after he climbed out.

Something similar was happening now in that open grave in the snow. Fanshawe was alone down there, thinking his thoughts, living through those moments by himself, and though I was present, the event was sealed off from me, as though I was not really there at all. I understood that this was Fanshawe's way of imagining his father's death. Again, it was a matter of pure chance: the open grave was there, and Fanshawe had felt it calling out to him. Stories happen only to those who are able to tell them, someone once said. In the same way, perhaps, experiences present themselves only to those who are able to have them. But this is a difficult point, and I can't be sure of any of it. I stood there waiting for Fanshawe to come up, trying to imagine what he was thinking, for a brief moment trying to see what he was seeing. Then I turned my head up to the darkening winter sky—and everything was a chaos of snow, rushing down on top of me.

By the time we started walking back to the car, the sun had set. We stumbled our way through the cemetery, not saying anything to each other. Several inches of snow had fallen, and it kept coming down, more and more heavily, as though it would never stop. We reached the car, climbed in, and then, against all our expectations, couldn't get moving. The back tires were stuck in a shallow ditch, and nothing we did made any difference. We pushed, we jostled, and still the tires spun with that horrible, futile noise. Half an hour went by, and then we gave up, reluctantly deciding to abandon the car. We hitch-hiked home in the storm, and another two hours went by before we finally made it back. It was only then that we learned that Fanshawe's father had died during the afternoon.

3

Several days went by before I found the courage to open the suitcases. I finished the article I was working on, I went to the movies, I accepted invitations I normally would have turned down. These tactics did not fool me, however. Too much depended on my response, and the possibility of being disappointed was something I did not want to face. There was no difference in my mind between giving the order to destroy Fanshawe's work and killing him with my own hands. I had been given the power to obliterate, to steal a body from its grave and tear it to pieces. It was an intolerable position to be in, and I wanted no part of it. As long as I left the suitcases untouched, my conscience would be spared. On the other hand, I had made a promise, and I knew that I could not delay forever. It was just at this point (gearing myself up, getting ready to do it) that a new dread took hold of me. If I did not want Fanshawe's work to be bad, I discovered, I also did not want it to be good. This is a difficult feeling for me to explain. Old rivalries no doubt had something to do with it, a desire not to be humbled by Fanshawe's brilliance—but there was also a feeling of being trapped. I had given my word. Once I opened the suitcases, I would become Fanshawe's spokesman—and I would go on speaking for him, whether I liked it or not. Both possibilities frightened me. To issue a death sentence was bad enough, but working for a dead man hardly seemed better. For several days I moved back and forth between these fears, unable to decide which one was worse. In the end, of course, I did open the suitcases. But by then it probably had less to do with Fanshawe than it did with Sophie. I wanted to see her again, and the sooner I got to work, the sooner I would have a reason to call her.

I am not planning to go into any details here. By now, everyone knows what Fanshawe's work is like. It has been read and discussed, there have been articles and studies, it has become public property. If there is anything to be said, it is only that it took me no more than an hour or two to understand that my feelings were quite beside the point. To care about words, to have a stake in what is written, to believe in the power of books—this overwhelms the rest, and beside it one's life becomes very small. I do not say this in order to congratulate myself or to put my actions in a better light. I was the first, but beyond that I see nothing to set me apart from anyone else. If Fanshawe's work had been any less than it was, my role would have been different—more important, perhaps, more crucial to the outcome of the story. But as it was, I was no more than an invisible instrument. Something had happened, and short of denying it, short of pretending I had not opened the suitcases, it would go on happening, knocking down whatever was in front of it, moving with a momentum of its own.

It took me about a week to digest and organize the material, to divide finished work from drafts, to gather the manuscripts into some semblance of chronological order. The earliest piece was a poem, dating from 1963 (when Fanshawe was sixteen), and the last was from 1976 (just one month before he disappeared). In all there were over a hundred poems, three novels (two short and one long), and five one-act plays—as well as thirteen notebooks, which contained a number of aborted pieces, sketches, jottings, remarks on the books Fanshawe was reading, and ideas for future projects. There were no letters, no diaries, no glimpses into Fanshawe's private life. But that was something I had expected. A man does not spend his time hiding from the world without making sure to cover his tracks. Still, I had thought that somewhere among all the papers there might be some mention of me—if only a letter of instruction or a notebook entry naming me his literary executor. But there was nothing. Fanshawe had left me entirely on my own.

I telephoned Sophie and arranged to have dinner with her the following night. Because I suggested a fashionable French restaurant (way beyond what I could afford), I think she was able to guess my response to Fanshawe's work. But beyond this hint of a celebration, I said as little

as I could. I wanted everything to advance at its own pace—
no abrupt moves, no premature gestures. I was already
certain about Fanshawe's work, but I was afraid to rush
into things with Sophie. Too much hinged on how I acted,
too much could be destroyed by blundering at the start.
Sophie and I were linked now, whether she knew it or not—
if only to the extent that we would be partners in promoting
Fanshawe's work. But I wanted more than that, and I
wanted Sophie to want it as well. Struggling against my
eagerness, I urged caution on myself, told myself to think
ahead.

She wore a black silk dress, tiny silver earrings, and had
swept back her hair to show the line of her neck. As she
walked into the restaurant and saw me sitting at the bar,
she gave me a warm, complicitous smile, as though telling
me she knew how beautiful she was, but at the same time
commenting on the weirdness of the occasion—savoring it
somehow, clearly alert to the outlandish implications of the
moment. I told her that she was stunning, and she answered
almost whimsically that this was her first night out since
Ben had been born—and that she had wanted to "look
different." After that, I stuck to business, trying to hang
back within myself. When we were led to our table and
given our seats (white tablecloth, heavy silverware, a red
tulip in a slender vase between us), I responded to her
second smile by talking about Fanshawe.

She did not seem surprised by anything I said. It was old

news for her, a fact that she had already come to terms with, and what I was telling her merely confirmed what she had known all along. Strangely enough, it did not seem to excite her. There was a wariness in her attitude that confused me, and for several minutes I was lost. Then, slowly, I began to understand that her feelings were not very different from my own. Fanshawe had disappeared from her life, and I saw that she might have good reason to resent the burden that had been imposed on her. By publishing Fanshawe's work, by devoting herself to a man who was no longer there, she would be forced to live in the past, and whatever future she might want to build for herself would be tainted by the role she had to play: the official widow, the dead writer's muse, the beautiful heroine in a tragic story. No one wants to be part of a fiction, and even less so if that fiction is real. Sophie was just twenty-six years old. She was too young to live through someone else, too intelligent not to want a life that was completely her own. The fact that she had loved Fanshawe was not the point. Fanshawe was dead, and it was time for her to leave him behind.

None of this was said in so many words. But the feeling was there, and it would have been senseless to ignore it. Given my own reservations, it was odd that I should have been the one to carry the torch, but I saw that if I didn't take hold of the thing and get it started, the job would never get done.

"You don't really have to get involved," I said. "We'll have to consult, of course, but that shouldn't take up much of your time. If you're willing to leave the decisions to me, I don't think it will be very bad at all."

"Of course I'll leave them to you," she said. "I don't know the first thing about any of this. If I tried to do it myself, I'd get lost within five minutes."

"The important thing is to know that we're on the same side," I said. "In the end, I suppose it boils down to whether or not you can trust me."

"I trust you," she said.

"I haven't given you any reason to," I said. "Not yet, in any case."

"I know that. But I trust you anyway."

"Just like that?"

"Yes. Just like that."

She smiled at me again, and for the rest of the dinner we said nothing more about Fanshawe's work. I had been planning to discuss it in detail—how best to begin, what publishers might be interested, what people to contact, and so on—but this no longer seemed important. Sophie was quite content not to think about it, and now that I had reassured her that she didn't have to, her playfulness gradually returned. After so many difficult months, she finally had a chance to forget some of it for a while, and I could see how determined she was to lose herself in the very simple pleasures of this moment: the restaurant, the food, the laughter of the people around us, the fact that she was here and not anywhere else. She wanted to be indulged in all this, and who was I not to go along with her?

I was in good form that night. Sophie inspired me, and it didn't take long for me to get warmed up. I cracked jokes, told stories, performed little tricks with the silverware. The woman was so beautiful that I had trouble keeping my eyes off her. I wanted to see her laugh, to see how her face would respond to what I said, to watch her eyes, to study her gestures. God knows what absurdities I came out with, but I did my best to detach myself, to bury my real motives under this onslaught of charm. That was the hard part. I knew that Sophie was lonely, that she wanted the comfort of a warm body beside her—but a quick roll in the hay was not what I was after, and if I moved too fast that was probably all it would turn out to be. At this early stage, Fanshawe was still there with us, the unspoken link, the invisible force that had brought us together. It would take some time before he disappeared, and until that happened, I found myself willing to wait.

All this created an exquisite tension. As the evening progressed, the most casual remarks became tinged with erotic overtones. Words were no longer simply words, but a curious code of silences, a way of speaking that continually moved around the thing that was being said. As long as we avoided the real subject, the spell would not be broken.

We both slipped naturally into this kind of banter, and it became all the more powerful because neither one of us abandoned the charade. We knew what we were doing, but at the same time we pretended not to. Thus my courtship of Sophie began—slowly, decorously, building by the smallest of increments.

After dinner we walked for twenty minutes or so in the late November darkness, then finished up the evening with drinks in a bar downtown. I smoked one cigarette after another, but that was the only clue to my tumult. Sophie talked for a while about her family in Minnesota, her three younger sisters, her arrival in New York eight years ago, her music, her teaching, her plan to go back to it next fall—but we were so firmly entrenched in our jocular mode by then that each remark became an excuse for additional laughter. It would have gone on, but there was the babysitter to think about, and so we finally cut it short at around midnight. I took her to the door of her apartment and made my last great effort of the evening.

"Thank you, doctor," Sophie said. "The operation was a success."

"My patients always survive," I said. "It's the laughing gas. I just turn on the valve, and little by little they get better."

"That gas might be habit-forming."

"That's the point. The patients keep coming back for more—sometimes two or three operations a week. How do you think I paid for my Park Avenue apartment and the summer place in France?"

"So there's a hidden motive."

"Absolutely. I'm driven by greed."

"Your practice must be booming."

"It was. But I'm more or less retired now. I'm down to one patient these days—and I'm not sure if she'll be coming back."

"She'll be back," Sophie said, with the coyest, most radiant smile I had ever seen. "You can count on it."

"That's good to hear," I said. "I'll have my secretary call her to schedule the next appointment."

"The sooner the better. With these long-term treatments, you can't waste a moment."

"Excellent advice. I'll remember to order a new supply of laughing gas."

"You do that, doctor. I really think I need it."

We smiled at each other again, and then I wrapped her up in a big bear hug, gave her a brief kiss on the lips, and got down the stairs as fast as I could.

I went straight home, realized that bed was out of the question, and then spent two hours in front of the television, watching a movie about Marco Polo. I finally conked out at around four, in the middle of a *Twilight Zone* rerun.

My first move was to contact Stuart Green, an editor at

one of the larger publishing houses. I didn't know him very well, but we had grown up in the same town, and his younger brother, Roger, had gone through school with me and Fanshawe. I guessed that Stuart would remember who Fanshawe was, and that seemed like a good way to get started. I had run into Stuart at various gatherings over the years, perhaps three or four times, and he had always been friendly, talking about the good old days (as he called them) and always promising to send my greetings to Roger the next time he saw him. I had no idea what to expect from Stuart, but he sounded happy enough to hear from me when I called. We arranged to meet at his office one afternoon that week.

It took him a few moments to place Fanshawe's name. It was familiar to him, he said, but he didn't know from where. I prodded his memory a bit, mentioned Roger and his friends, and then it suddenly came back to him. "Yes, yes, of course," he said. "Fanshawe. That extraordinary little boy. Roger used to insist that he would grow up to be President." That's the one, I said, and then I told him the story.

Stuart was a rather prissy fellow, a Harvard type who wore bow ties and tweed jackets, and though at bottom he was little more than a company man, in the publishing world he was what passed for an intellectual. He had done well for himself so far—a senior editor in his early thirties, a solid and responsible young worker—and there was no question that he was on the rise. I say all this only to prove that he was not someone who would be automatically susceptible to the kind of story I was telling. There was very little romance in him, very little that was not cautious and business-like—but I could feel that he was interested, and as I went on talking, he even seemed to become excited.

He had nothing to lose, of course. If Fanshawe's work didn't appeal to him, it would be simple enough for him to turn it down. Rejections were the heart of his job, and he wouldn't have to think twice about it. On the other hand, if Fanshawe was the writer I said he was, then publishing him could only help Stuart's reputation. He would share in the glory of having discovered an unknown American genius, and he would be able to live off this coup for years.

I handed him the manuscript of Fanshawe's big novel. In the end, I said, it would have to be all or nothing—the poems, the plays, the other two novels—but this was Fanshawe's major work, and it was logical that it should come first. I was referring to *Neverland*, of course. Stuart said that he liked the title, but when he asked me to describe the book, I said that I'd rather not, that I thought it would be better if he found out for himself. He raised an eyebrow in response (a trick he had probably learned during his year at Oxford), as if to imply that I shouldn't play games with him. I wasn't, as far as I could tell. It was just that I didn't want to coerce him. The book could do the work itself, and I saw no reason to deny him the pleasure of entering it cold: with no map, no compass, no one to lead him by the hand.

It took three weeks for him to get back to me. The news was neither good nor bad, but it seemed hopeful. There was probably enough support among the editors to get the book through, Stuart said, but before they made the final decision they wanted to have a look at the other material. I had been expecting that—a certain prudence, playing it close to the vest—and told Stuart that I would come around to drop off the manuscripts the following afternoon.

"It's a strange book," he said, pointing to the copy of *Neverland* on his desk. "Not at all your typical novel, you know. Not your typical anything. It's still not clear that we're going ahead with it, but if we do, publishing it will be something of a risk."

"I know that," I said. "But that's what makes it interesting."

"The real pity is that Fanshawe isn't around. I'd love to be able to work with him. There are things in the book that should be changed, I think, certain passages that should be cut. It would make the book even stronger."

"That's just editor's pride," I said. "It's hard for you to see a manuscript and not want to attack it with a red pencil. The fact is, I think the parts you object to now will eventually make sense to you, and you'll be glad you weren't able to touch them."

"Time will tell," said Stuart, not ready to concede the

point. "But there's no question," he went on, "no question
that the man could write. I read the book more than two
weeks ago, and it's been with me ever since. I can't get it out
of my head. It keeps coming back to me, and always at the
strangest moments. Stepping out of the shower, walking
down the street, crawling into bed at night—whenever I'm
not consciously thinking about anything. That doesn't
happen very often, you know. You read so many books in
this job that they all tend to blur together. But Fanshawe's
book stands out. There's something powerful about it, and
the oddest thing is that I don't even know what it is."

"That's probably the real test," I said. "The same thing
happened to me. The book gets stuck somewhere in the
brain, and you can't get rid of it."

"And what about the other stuff?"

"Same thing," I said. "You can't stop thinking about it."

Stuart shook his head, and for the first time I saw that he
was honestly impressed. It lasted no more than a moment,
but in that moment his arrogance and posturing suddenly
disappeared, and I almost found myself wanting to like him.

"I think we might be on to something," he said. "If what
you say is true, then I really think we might be on to
something."

We were, and as things turned out, perhaps even more
than Stuart had imagined. *Neverland* was accepted later
that month, with an option on the other books as well. My
quarter of the advance was enough to buy me some time,

and I used it to work on an edition of the poems. I also went to a number of directors to see if there was any interest in doing the plays. Eventually, this came off, too, and a production of three one-acts was planned for a small downtown theater—to open about six weeks after *Neverland* was published. In the meantime, I persuaded the editor of one of the bigger magazines I occasionally wrote for to let me do an article on Fanshawe. It turned out to be a long, rather exotic piece, and at the time I felt it was one of the best things I had ever written. The article was scheduled to appear two months before the publication of *Neverland*—and suddenly it seemed as though everything was happening at once.

I admit that I got caught up in it all. One thing kept leading to another, and before I knew it a small industry had been set in motion. It was a kind of delirium, I think. I felt like an engineer, pushing buttons and pulling levers, scrambling from valve chambers to circuit boxes, adjusting a part here, devising an improvement there, listening to the contraption hum and chug and purr, oblivious to everything but the din of my brainchild. I was the mad scientist who had invented the great hocus-pocus machine, and the more smoke that poured from it, the more noise it produced, the happier I was.

Perhaps that was inevitable; perhaps I needed to be a little mad in order to get started. Given the strain of reconciling myself to the project, it was probably necessary for me to equate Fanshawe's success with my own. I had stumbled onto a cause, a thing that justified me and made me feel important, and the more fully I disappeared into my ambitions for Fanshawe, the more sharply I came into focus for myself. This is not an excuse; it is merely a description of what happened. Hindsight tells me that I was looking for trouble, but at the time I knew nothing about it. More important, even if I had known, I doubt that it would have made a difference.

Underneath it all was the desire to stay in touch with Sophie. As time went on, it became perfectly natural for me to call her three or four times a week, to see her for lunch, to stop by for an afternoon stroll through the neighborhood with Ben. I introduced her to Stuart Green, invited her along to meet the theater director, found her a lawyer to handle contracts and other legal matters. Sophie took all this in her stride, treating these encounters more as social occasions than as business talks, making it clear to the people we saw that I was the one in charge. I sensed that she was determined not to feel indebted to Fanshawe, that whatever happened or did not happen, she would continue to keep her distance from it. The money made her happy, of course, but she never really connected it to Fanshawe's work. It was an unlikely gift, a winning lottery ticket that had dropped from the sky, and that was all. Sophie saw through the whirlwind from the very start. She understood the fundamental absurdity of the situation, and because there was no greed in her, no impulse to press her own advantage, she did not lose her head.

I worked hard at courting her. No doubt my motives were transparent, but perhaps that was to the good. Sophie knew that I had fallen in love with her, and the fact that I did not pounce on her, that I did not force her to declare her feelings for me, probably did more to convince her of my seriousness than anything else. Still, I could not wait forever. Discretion has its role, but too much of it can be fatal. A moment came when I could feel that we were no longer jousting with each other, that things between us had already been settled. In thinking about this moment now, I am tempted to use the traditional language of love. I want to talk in metaphors of heat, of burning, of barriers melting down in the face of irresistible passions. I am aware of how overblown these terms might sound, but in the end I believe they are accurate. Everything had changed for me, and words that I had never understood before suddenly began to make sense. This came as a revelation, and when I finally had time to absorb it, I wondered how I had managed to live so long without learning this simple thing. I am not talking about desire so much as knowledge, the discovery that two people, through desire, can create a thing more powerful than either of them can create alone. This knowledge changed me, I think, and actually made me feel more human. By belonging to Sophie, I began to feel as though I belonged to everyone else as well. My true place in the world, it turned out, was somewhere beyond myself, and if that place was inside me, it was also unlocatable. This was the tiny hole between self and not-self, and for the first time in my life I saw this nowhere as the exact center of the world.

It happened to be my thirtieth birthday. I had known Sophie for about three months by then, and she insisted on making an evening of it. I was reluctant at first, never having paid much attention to birthdays, but Sophie's sense of occasion finally won me over. She bought me an expensive, illustrated edition of *Moby Dick*, took me to dinner in a good restaurant, and then ushered me along to a performance of *Boris Godunov* at the Met. For once, I let myself go with it, not trying to second-guess my happiness, not trying to stay ahead of myself or outmaneuver my feelings. Perhaps I was beginning to sense a new boldness in Sophie; perhaps she was making it known to me that she had decided things for herself, that it was too late now for either one of us to back off. Whatever it was, that was the night when everything changed, when there was no longer any question of what we were going to do. We returned to her apartment at eleven-thirty, Sophie paid the drowsy babysitter, and then we tiptoed into Ben's room and stood there for a while watching him as he slept in his crib. I remember distinctly that neither one of us said anything, that the only sound I could hear was the faint gurgling of Ben's breath. We leaned over the bars and studied the shape of his little body—lying on his stomach, legs tucked under him, ass in the air, two or three fingers stuck in his mouth. It seemed to go on for a long time, but I doubt it was more than a minute or two. Then, without any warning, we both straightened up, turned towards each other, and began to kiss. After that, it is difficult for me to speak of what happened. Such things have little to do with words, so little, in fact, that it seems almost pointless to try to express them. If anything, I would say that we were falling into each other, that we were falling so fast and so far that nothing could catch us. Again, I lapse into metaphor. But that is probably beside the point. For whether or not I can talk about it does not change the truth of what happened. The fact is, there never was such a kiss, and in all my life I doubt there can ever be such a kiss again.

4

I spent that night in Sophie's bed, and from then on it
became impossible to leave it. I would go back to my own
apartment during the day to work, but every evening I
would return to Sophie. I became a part of the household—
shopping for dinner, changing Ben's diapers, taking out the
garbage—living more intimately with another person than I
had ever lived before. Months went by, and to my constant
bewilderment, I discovered that I had a talent for this kind
of life. I had been born to be with Sophie, and little by little
I could feel myself becoming stronger, could feel her making
me better than I had been. It was strange how Fanshawe
had brought us together. If not for his disappearance, none
of this would have happened. I owed him a debt, but other
than doing what I could for his work, I had no chance to
pay it back.

My article was published, and it seemed to have the
desired effect. Stuart Green called to say that it was a
"great boost"—which I gathered to mean that he felt more
secure now in having accepted the book. With all the
interest the article had generated, Fanshawe no longer

seemed like such a long shot. Then *Neverland* came out, and the reviews were uniformly good, some of them extraordinary. It was all that one could have hoped for. This was the fairy tale that every writer dreams about, and I admit that even I was a little shocked. Such things are not supposed to happen in the real world. Only a few weeks after publication, sales were greater than had been expected for the whole edition. A second printing eventually went to press, there were ads placed in newspapers and magazines, and then the book was sold to a paperback company for republication the following year. I don't mean to imply that the book was a bestseller by commercial standards or that Sophie was on her way to becoming a millionaire, but given the seriousness and difficulty of Fanshawe's work, and given the public's tendency to stay away from such work, it was a success beyond anything we had imagined possible.

In some sense, this is where the story should end. The young genius is dead, but his work will live on, his name will be remembered for years to come. His childhood friend has rescued the beautiful young widow, and the two of them will live happily ever after. That would seem to wrap it up, with nothing left but a final curtain call. But it turns out that this is only the beginning. What I have written so far is no more than a prelude, a quick synopsis of everything that comes before the story I have to tell. If there were no more to it than this, there would be nothing at all—for nothing would have compelled me to begin. Only darkness has the power to make a man open his heart to the world, and darkness is what surrounds me whenever I think of what happened. If courage is needed to write about it, I also know that writing about it is the one chance I have to escape. But I doubt this will happen, not even if I manage to tell the truth. Stories without endings can do nothing but go on forever, and to be caught in one means that you must die before your part in it is played out. My only hope is that there is an end to what I am about to say, that somewhere I will find a break in the darkness. This hope is what I define as courage, but whether there is reason to hope is another question entirely.

It was about three weeks after the plays had opened. I spent the night at Sophie's apartment as usual, and in the morning I went uptown to my place to do some work. I remember that I was supposed to be finishing a piece on four or five books of poetry—one of those frustrating, hodge-podge reviews—and I was having trouble concentrating. My mind kept wandering away from the books on my desk, and every five minutes or so I would pop up from my chair and pace about the room. A strange story had been reported to me by Stuart Green the day before, and it was hard for me to stop thinking about it. According to Stuart, people were beginning to say that there was no such person as Fanshawe. The rumor was that I had invented him to perpetrate a hoax and had actually written the books myself. My first response was to laugh, and I made some crack about how Shakespeare hadn't written any plays either. But now that I had given some thought to it, I didn't know whether to feel insulted or flattered by this talk. Did people not trust me to tell the truth? Why would I go to the trouble of creating an entire body of work and then not want to take credit for it? And yet—did people really think I was capable of writing a book as good as *Neverland*? I realized that once all of Fanshawe's manuscripts had been published, it would be perfectly possible for me to write another book or two under his name—to do the work myself and yet pass it off as his. I was not planning to do this, of course, but the mere thought of it opened up certain bizarre and intriguing notions to me: what it means when a writer puts his name on a book, why some writers choose to hide behind a pseudonym, whether or not a writer has a real life anyway. It struck me that writing under another name might be something I would enjoy—to invent a secret identity for myself—and I wondered why I found this idea so attractive. One thought kept leading me to another, and by the time the subject was exhausted, I discovered that I had squandered most of the morning.

Eleven-thirty rolled around—the hour of the mail—and I made my ritual excursion down the elevator to see if there was anything in my box. This was always a crucial moment of the day for me, and I found it impossible to approach it calmly. There was always the hope that good news would be sitting there—an unexpected check, an offer of work, a letter that would somehow change my life—and by now the habit of anticipation was so much a part of me that I could scarcely look at my mailbox without getting a rush. This was my hiding place, the one spot in the world that was purely my own. And yet it linked me to the rest of the world, and in its magic darkness there was the power to make things happen.

There was only one letter for me that day. It came in a plain white envelope with a New York postmark and had no return address. The handwriting was unfamiliar to me (my name and address were printed out in block letters), and I couldn't even begin to guess who it was from. I opened the envelope in the elevator—and it was then, standing there on my way to the ninth floor, that the world fell on top of me.

"Don't be angry with me for writing to you," the letter began. "At the risk of causing you heart failure, I wanted to send you one last word—to thank you for what you have done. I knew that you were the person to ask, but things have turned out even better than I thought they would. You have gone beyond the possible, and I am in your debt. Sophie and the child will be taken care of, and because of that I can live with a clear conscience.

"I'm not going to explain myself here. In spite of this letter, I want you to go on thinking of me as dead. Nothing is more important than that, and you must not tell anyone that you've heard from me. I am not going to be found, and to speak of it would only lead to more trouble than it's worth. Above all, say nothing to Sophie. Make her divorce me, and then marry her as soon as you can. I trust you to do that—and I give you my blessings. The child needs a father, and you're the only one I can count on.

"I want you to understand that I haven't lost my mind. I made certain decisions that were necessary, and though people have suffered, leaving was the best and kindest thing I have ever done.

"Seven years from the day of my disappearance will be the day of my death. I have passed judgment on myself, and no appeals will be heard.

"I beg you not to look for me. I have no desire to be found, and it seems to me that I have the right to live the rest of my life as I see fit. Threats are repugnant to me—but I have no choice but to give you this warning: if by some miracle you manage to track me down, I will kill you.

"I'm pleased that so much interest has been taken in my writing. I never had the slightest inkling that anything like this could happen. But it all seems so far away from me now. Writing books belongs to another life, and to think about it now leaves me cold. I will never try to claim any of the money—and I gladly give it to you and Sophie. Writing was an illness that plagued me for a long time, but now I have recovered from it.

"Rest assured that I won't be in touch again. You are free of me now, and I wish you a long and happy life. How much better that everything should come to this. You are my friend, and my one hope is that you will always be who you are. With me it's another story. Wish me luck."

There was no signature at the bottom of the letter, and for the next hour or two I tried to persuade myself that it was a prank. If Fanshawe had written it, why would he have neglected to sign his name? I clung to this as evidence of a trick, desperately looking for an excuse to deny what had happened. But this optimism did not last very long, and little by little I forced myself to face the facts. There could be any number of reasons for the name to be left out, and the more I thought about it, the more clearly I saw that this was precisely why the letter should be considered genuine. A prankster would make a special point of including the name, but the real person would not think twice about it: only someone not out to deceive would have the self-assurance to make such an apparent mistake. And then there were the final sentences of the letter: " . . . remain who you are. With me it's another story." Did this mean that Fanshawe had become someone else? Unquestionably, he was living under another name—but how was he living—and where? The New York postmark was something of a clue, perhaps, but it just as easily could have been a blind, a bit of false information to throw me off his track. Fanshawe had been extremely careful. I read the letter over and over, trying to pull it apart, looking for an opening, a way to read between the lines—but nothing came of it. The letter was opaque, a block of darkness that thwarted every attempt to get inside it. In the end I gave up, put the letter in a drawer of my desk, and admitted that I was lost, that nothing would ever be the same for me again.

What bothered me most, I think, was my own stupidity. Looking back on it now, I saw that all the facts had been given to me at the start—as early as my first meeting with Sophie. For years Fanshawe publishes nothing, then he tells his wife what to do if anything should happen to him (contact me, get his work published), and then he vanishes. It was all so obvious. The man wanted to leave, and he left. He simply got up one day and walked out on his pregnant wife, and because she trusted him, because it was inconceivable to her that he would do such a thing, she had no choice but to think he was dead. Sophie had deluded herself, but given the situation, it was hard to see how she could have done otherwise. I had no such excuse. Not once from the very beginning had I thought things through for myself. I had jumped right in with her, had rejoiced in accepting her misreading of the facts, and then had stopped thinking altogether. People have been shot for smaller crimes than that.

The days went by. All my instincts told me to confide in Sophie, to share the letter with her, and yet I couldn't bring myself to do it. I was too afraid, too uncertain as to how she would react. In my stronger moods, I argued to myself that keeping silent was the only way to protect her. What possible good would it do for her to know that Fanshawe

had walked out on her? She would blame herself for what
had happened, and I didn't want her to be hurt. Underneath this noble silence, however, there was a second
silence of panic and fear. Fanshawe was alive—and if I let
Sophie know it, what would this knowledge do to us? The
thought that Sophie might want him back was too much for
me, and I did not have the courage to risk finding out. This
was perhaps my greatest failure of all. If I had believed
enough in Sophie's love for me, I would have been willing to
risk anything. But at the time there seemed to be no other
choice, and so I did what Fanshawe had asked me to do—
not for him, but for myself. I locked up the secret inside me
and learned to hold my tongue.

A few more days went by, and then I proposed marriage
to Sophie. We had talked about it before, but this time I
took it out of the realm of talk, making it clear to her that
I meant business. I realized that I was acting out of
character (humorless, inflexible), but I couldn't help myself. The uncertainty of the situation was impossible to live
with, and I felt that I had to resolve things right then and
there. Sophie noticed this change in me, of course, but since
she didn't know the reason for it, she interpreted it as an
excess of passion—the behavior of a nervous, overly ardent
male, panting after the thing he wanted most (which was
also true). Yes, she said, she would marry me. Did I ever
really think she would turn me down?

"And I want to adopt Ben, too," I said. "I want him to

have my name. It's important that he grow up thinking of me as his father."

Sophie answered that she wouldn't have it any other way. It was the only thing that made sense—for all three of us.

"And I want it to happen soon," I went on, "as soon as possible. In New York, you couldn't get a divorce for a year—and that's too long, I couldn't stand waiting that long. But there are other places. Alabama, Nevada, Mexico, God knows where. We could go off on a vacation, and by the time we got back, you'd be free to marry me."

Sophie said that she liked the way that sounded—"free to marry me." If it meant going somewhere for a while, she would go, she said, she would go anywhere I wanted.

"After all," I said, "he's been gone for more than a year now, almost a year and a half. It takes seven years before a dead person can be declared officially dead. Things happen, life moves on. Just think: we've known each other for almost a year."

"To be precise," Sophie answered, "you walked through that door for the first time on November twenty-fifth, nineteen-seventy-six. In eight more days it will be exactly a year."

"You remember."

"Of course I remember. It was the most important day of my life."

We took a plane to Birmingham, Alabama on November twenty-seventh and were back in New York by the first

week of December. On the eleventh we were married in City
Hall, and afterward we went to a drunken dinner with
about twenty of our friends. We spent that night at the
Plaza, ordered a room service breakfast in the morning,
and later that day flew to Minnesota with Ben. On the
eighteenth, Sophie's parents gave us a wedding party at
their house, and on the night of the twenty-fourth we
celebrated Norwegian Christmas. Two days later, Sophie
and I left the snow and went to Bermuda for a week and a
half, then returned to Minnesota to fetch Ben. Our plan was
to start looking for a new apartment as soon as we got back
to New York. Somewhere over western Pennsylvania,
about an hour into the flight, Ben peed through his diapers
onto my lap. When I showed him the large dark spot on my
pants, he laughed, clapped his hands together, and then,
looking straight into my eyes, called me Da for the first
time.

5

I dug into the present. Several months passed, and little by little it began to seem possible that I would survive. This was life in a foxhole, but Sophie and Ben were down there with me, and that was all I really wanted. As long as I remembered not to look up, the danger could not touch us.

We moved to an apartment on Riverside Drive in February. Settling in carried us through to mid-spring, and I had little chance to dwell on Fanshawe. If the letter did not vanish from my thoughts altogether, it no longer posed the same threat. I was secure with Sophie now, and I felt that nothing could break us apart—not even Fanshawe, not even Fanshawe in the flesh. Or so it appeared to me then, whenever I happened to think of it. I understand now how badly I was deceiving myself, but I did not find that out until much later. By definition, a thought is something you are aware of. The fact that I did not once stop thinking about Fanshawe, that he was inside me day and night for all those months, was unknown to me at the time. And if you are not aware of having a thought, is it legitimate to say that you are thinking? I was haunted, perhaps, I was even possessed—but there were no signs of it, no clues to tell me what was happening.

Daily life was full for me now. I hardly noticed that I was doing less work than I had in years. I had no job to go off to in the morning, and since Sophie and Ben were in the apartment with me, it was not very difficult to find excuses for avoiding my desk. My work schedule grew slack. Instead of beginning at nine sharp every day, I sometimes didn't make it to my little room until eleven or eleven-thirty. On top of that, Sophie's presence in the house was a constant temptation. Ben still took one or two naps a day, and in those quiet hours while he slept, it was hard for me not to think about her body. More often than not, we wound up making love. Sophie was just as hungry for it as I was, and as the weeks passed, the house was slowly eroticized, transformed into a domain of sexual possibilities. The nether world rose up to the surface. Each room acquired its own memory, each spot evoked a different moment, so that even in the calm of practical life, a particular patch of carpet, say, or the threshold of a particular door, was no longer strictly a thing but a sensation, an echo of our erotic life. We had entered the paradox of desire. Our need for each other was inexhaustible, and the more it was fulfilled, the more it seemed to grow.

Every now and then, Sophie talked of looking for a job, but neither one of us felt any urgency about it. Our money was holding up well, and we even managed to put away quite

a bit. Fanshawe's next book, *Miracles*, was in the works, and
the advance from the contract had been heftier than the one
from *Neverland*. According to the schedule that Stuart and
I had charted out, the poems would come six months after
Miracles, then Fanshawe's earliest novel, *Blackouts*, and
last of all the plays. Royalties from *Neverland* started coming in that March, and with checks suddenly arriving for one
thing and another, all money problems evaporated. Like
everything else that seemed to be happening, this was a new
experience for me. For the past eight or nine years, my life
had been a constant scrambling act, a frantic lunge from one
paltry article to the next, and I had considered myself lucky
whenever I could see ahead for more than a month or two.
Care was embedded inside me; it was part of my blood, my
corpuscles, and I hardly knew what it was to breathe without
wondering if I could afford to pay the gas bill. Now, for the
first time since I had gone out on my own, I realized that I
didn't have to think about these things anymore. One morning, as I sat at my desk struggling over the final sentence of
an article, groping for a phrase that was not there, it gradually dawned on me that I had been given a second chance.
I could give this up and start again. I no longer had to write
articles. I could move on to other things, begin to do the work
I had always wanted to do. This was my chance to save
myself, and I decided I'd be a fool not to take it.

More weeks passed. I went into my room every morning,
but nothing happened. Theoretically, I felt inspired, and

whenever I was not working, my head was filled with ideas. But each time I sat down to put something on paper, my thoughts seemed to vanish. Words died the moment I lifted my pen. I started a number of projects, but nothing really took hold, and one by one I dropped them. I looked for excuses to explain why I couldn't get going. That was no problem, and before long I had come up with a whole litany: the adjustment to married life, the responsibilities of fatherhood, my new workroom (which seemed too cramped), the old habit of writing for a deadline, Sophie's body, the sudden windfall—everything. For several days, I even toyed with the idea of writing a detective novel, but then I got stuck with the plot and couldn't fit all the pieces together. I let my mind drift without purpose, hoping to persuade myself that idleness was proof of gathering strength, a sign that something was about to happen. For more than a month, the only thing I did was copy out passages from books. One of them, from Spinoza, I tacked onto my wall: "And when he dreams he does not want to write, he does not have the power to dream he wants to write; and when he dreams he wants to write, he does not have the power to dream he does not want to write."

It's possible that I would have worked my way out of this slump. Whether it was a permanent condition or a passing phase is still unclear to me. My gut feeling is that for a time I was truly lost, floundering desperately inside myself, but I do not think this means my case was hopeless. Things were happening to me. I was living through great changes, and it was still too early to tell where they were going to lead. Then, unexpectedly, a solution presented itself. If that is too favorable a word, I will call it a compromise. Whatever it was, I put up very little resistance to it. It came at a vulnerable time for me, and my judgment was not all it should have been. This was my second crucial mistake, and it followed directly from the first.

I was having lunch with Stuart one day near his office on the Upper East Side. Midway through the meal, he brought up the Fanshawe rumors again, and for the first time it occurred to me that he was actually beginning to have doubts. The subject was so fascinating to him that he couldn't stay away from it. His manner was arch, mockingly conspiratorial, but underneath the pose I began to suspect that he was trying to trap me into a confession. I played along with him for a while, and then, growing tired of the game, said that the one foolproof method for settling the question was to commission a biography. I made this remark in all innocence (as a logical point, not as a suggestion), but it seemed to strike Stuart as a splendid idea. He began to gush: of course, of course, the Fanshawe myth explained, perfectly obvious, of course, the true story at last. In a matter of minutes he had the whole thing figured out. I would write the book. It would appear after all of Fanshawe's work had been published, and I could have as much time as I wanted—two years, three years, whatever. It would have to be an extraordinary book, Stuart added, a book equal to Fanshawe himself, but he had great confidence in me, and he knew I could do the job. The proposal caught me off guard, and I treated it as a joke. But Stuart was serious; he wouldn't let me turn him down. Give it some thought, he said, and then tell me how you feel. I remained skeptical, but to be polite I told him I would think about it. We agreed that I would give him a final answer by the end of the month.

I discussed it with Sophie that night, but since I couldn't talk to her honestly, the conversation was not much help to me.

"It's up to you," she said. "If you want to do it, I think you should go ahead."

"It doesn't bother you?"

"No. At least I don't think so. It's already occurred to me that sooner or later there would be a book about him. If it has to happen, then better it should be by you than by someone else."

"I'd have to write about you and Fanshawe. It might be strange."

"A few pages will be enough. As long as you're the one who's writing them, I'm not really worried."

"Maybe," I said, not knowing how to continue. "The toughest question, I suppose, is whether I want to get so involved in thinking about Fanshawe. Maybe it's time to let him fade away."

"It's your decision. But the fact is, you could do this book better than anyone else. And it doesn't have to be a straight biography, you know. You could do something more interesting."

"Like what?"

"I don't know, something more personal, more gripping. The story of your friendship. It could be as much about you as about him."

"Maybe. At least it's an idea. The thing that puzzles me is how you can be so calm about it."

"Because I'm married to you and I love you, that's how. If you decide it's something you want to do, then I'm for it. I'm not blind, after all. I know you've been having trouble with your work, and I sometimes feel that I'm to blame for it. Maybe this is the kind of project you need to get started again."

I had secretly been counting on Sophie to make the decision for me, assuming she would object, assuming we would talk about it once and that would be the end of it. But just the opposite had happened. I had backed myself into a corner, and my courage suddenly failed me. I let a couple of days go by, and then I called Stuart and told him I would do the book. This got me another free lunch, and after that I was on my own.

There was never any question of telling the truth.

Fanshawe had to be dead, or else the book would make no sense. Not only would I have to leave the letter out, but I would have to pretend that it had never been written. I make no bones about what I was planning to do. It was clear to me from the beginning, and I plunged into it with deceit in my heart. The book was a work of fiction. Even though it was based on facts, it could tell nothing but lies. I signed the contract, and afterwards I felt like a man who had signed away his soul.

I wandered in my mind for several weeks, looking for a way to begin. Every life is inexplicable, I kept telling myself. No matter how many facts are told, no matter how many details are given, the essential thing resists telling. To say that so and so was born here and went there, that he did this and did that, that he married this woman and had these children, that he lived, that he died, that he left behind these books or this battle or that bridge—none of that tells us very much. We all want to be told stories, and we listen to them in the same way we did when we were young. We imagine the real story inside the words, and to do this we substitute ourselves for the person in the story, pretending that we can understand him because we understand ourselves. This is a deception. We exist for ourselves, perhaps, and at times we even have a glimmer of who we are, but in the end we can never be sure, and as our lives go on, we become more and more opaque to ourselves, more and more aware of our own incoherence. No one can cross the boundary into another—for the simple reason that no one can gain access to himself.

I thought back to something that had happened to me eight years earlier, in June of 1970. Short of money, and with no immediate prospects for the summer, I took a temporary job as a census-taker in Harlem. There were about twenty of us in the group, a commando corps of field workers hired to track down people who had not responded to the questionnaires sent out in the mail. We trained for several days in a dusty second-floor loft across from the Apollo Theatre, and then, having mastered the intricacies of the forms and the basic rules of census-taker etiquette, dispersed into the neighborhood with our red, white, and blue shoulder bags to knock on doors, ask questions, and return with the facts. The first place I went to turned out to be the headquarters of a numbers operation. The door opened a sliver, a head poked out (behind it I could see a dozen men in a bare room writing on long picnic tables), and I was politely told that they weren't interested. That seemed to set the tone. In one apartment I talked with a half-blind woman whose parents had been slaves. Twenty minutes into the interview, it finally dawned on her that I wasn't black, and she started cackling with laughter. She had suspected it all long, she said, since my voice was funny, but she had trouble believing it. I was the first white person who had ever been inside her house. In another apartment, I came upon a household of eleven people, none of them older than twenty-two. But for the most part no one was there. And when they were, they wouldn't talk to me or let me in. Summer came, and the streets grew hot and humid, intolerable in the way that only New York can be. I would begin my rounds early, blundering stupidly from house to house, feeling more and more like a man from the moon. I finally spoke to the supervisor (a fast-talking black man who wore silk ascots and a sapphire ring) and explained my problem to him. It was then that I learned what was really expected of me. This man was paid a certain amount for each form a member of his crew turned in. The better our results, the more money would go into his pocket. "I'm not telling you what to do," he said, "but it seems to me that if you've given it an honest shot, then you shouldn't feel too bad."

"Just give up?" I asked.

"On the other hand," he continued philosophically, "the government wants completed forms. The more forms they get, the better they're going to feel. Now I know you're an intelligent boy, and I know you don't get five when you put two and two together. Just because a door doesn't open when you knock on it doesn't mean that nobody's there. You've got to use your imagination, my friend. After all, we don't want the government to be unhappy, do we?"

The job became considerably easier after that, but it was no longer the same job. My field work had turned into desk work, and instead of an investigator I was now an inventor. Every day or two, I stopped by the office to pick up a new batch of forms and turn in the ones I had finished, but other than that I didn't have to leave my apartment. I don't know how many people I invented—but there must have been hundreds of them, perhaps thousands. I would sit in my room with the fan blowing in my face and a cold towel wrapped around my neck, filling out questionnaires as fast as my hand could write. I went in for big households—six, eight, ten children—and took special pride in concocting odd and complicated networks of relationships, drawing on all the possible combinations: parents, children, cousins, uncles, aunts, grandparents, common law spouses, step-children, half-brothers, half-sisters, and friends. Most of all, there was the pleasure of making up names. At times I had to curb my impulse towards the outlandish—the fiercely comical, the pun, the dirty word—but for the most part I was content to stay within the bounds of realism. When my imagination flagged, there were certain mechanical devices to fall back on: the colors (Brown, White, Black, Green, Gray, Blue), the Presidents (Washington, Adams, Jefferson, Fillmore, Pierce), fictional characters (Finn, Starbuck, Dimmsdale, Budd). I liked names associated with the sky (Orville Wright, Amelia Earhart), with silent humor (Keaton, Langdon, Lloyd), with long homeruns (Killebrew, Mantle, Mays), and with music (Schubert, Ives, Armstrong). Occasionally, I would dredge up the names of distant relatives or old school friends, and once I even used an anagram of my own.

It was a childish thing to be doing, but I had no qualms. Nor was it hard to justify. The supervisor would not object; the people who actually lived at the addresses on the forms would not object (they did not want to be bothered, especially not by a white boy snooping into their personal business); and the government would not object, since what it did not know could not hurt it, and certainly no more than it was already hurting itself. I even went so far as to defend my preference for large families on political grounds: the greater the poor population, the more obligated the government would feel to spend money on it. This was the dead souls scam with an American twist, and my conscience was clear.

That was on one level. At the heart of it was the simple fact that I was enjoying myself. It gave me pleasure to pluck names out of thin air, to invent lives that had never existed, that never would exist. It was not precisely like making up characters in a story, but something grander, something far more unsettling. Everyone knows that stories are imaginary. Whatever effect they might have on us, we know they are not true, even when they tell us truths more important than the ones we can find elsewhere. As opposed to the story writer, I was offering my creations directly to the real world, and therefore it seemed possible to me that they could affect this real world in a real way, that they could eventually become a part of the real itself. No writer could ask for more than that.

All this came back to me when I sat down to write about Fanshawe. Once, I had given birth to a thousand imaginary souls. Now, eight years later, I was going to take a living man and put him in his grave. I was the chief mourner and officiating clergyman at this mock funeral, and my job was to speak the right words, to say the thing that everyone wanted to hear. The two actions were opposite and identical, mirror images of one another. But this hardly consoled me. The first fraud had been a joke, no more than a youthful adventure, whereas the second fraud was serious, a dark and frightening thing. I was digging a grave, after all, and there were times when I began to wonder if I was not digging my own.

Lives make no sense, I argued. A man lives and then he dies, and what happens in between makes no sense. I thought of the story of La Chère, a soldier who took part in one of the earliest French expeditions to America. In 1562, Jean Ribaut left behind a number of men at Port Royal (near Hilton Head, South Carolina) under the command of Albert de Pierra, a madman who ruled through terror and violence. "He hanged with his own hands a drummer who had fallen under his displeasure," Francis Parkman writes, "and banished a soldier, named La Chère, to a solitary island, three leagues from the fort, where he left him to starve." Albert was eventually murdered in an uprising by his men, and the half-dead La Chère was rescued from the island. One would think that La Chère was now safe, that having lived through his terrible punishment he would be exempt from further catastrophe. But nothing is that simple. There are no odds to beat, no rules to set a limit on bad luck, and at each moment we begin again, as ripe for a low blow as we were the moment before. Things collapsed at the settlement. The men had no talent for coping with the wilderness, and famine and homesickness took over. Using a few makeshift tools, they spent all their energies on building a ship "worthy of Robinson Crusoe" to get them back to France. On the Atlantic, another catastrophe: there was no wind, their food and water ran out. The men began to eat their shoes and leather jerkins, some drank sea water in desperation, and several died. Then came the inevitable descent into cannibalism. "The lot was cast," Parkman notes, "and it fell on La Chère, the same wretched man whom Albert had doomed to starvation on a lonely island. They killed him, and with ravenous avidity portioned out his flesh. The hideous repast sustained them till land rose in sight, when, it is said, in a delirium of joy, they could no longer steer their vessel, but let her drift at the will of the tide. A small English bark bore down upon them, took them all on board, and, after landing the feeblest, carried the rest prisoners to Queen Elizabeth."

I use La Chère only as an example. As destinies go, his is by no means strange—perhaps it is even blander than most. At least he travelled along a straight line, and that in itself is rare, almost a blessing. In general, lives seem to veer abruptly from one thing to another, to jostle and bump, to squirm. A person heads in one direction, turns sharply in mid-course, stalls, drifts, starts up again. Nothing is ever known, and inevitably we come to a place quite different from the one we set out for. In my first year as a student at Columbia, I walked by a bust of Lorenzo Da Ponte every day on my way to class. I knew him vaguely as Mozart's librettist, but then I learned that he had also been the first Italian professor at Columbia. The one thing seemed incompatible with the other, and so I decided to look into it, curious to know how one man could wind up living two such different lives. As it turned out, Da Ponte lived five or six. He was born Emmanuele Conegliano in 1749, the son of a Jewish leather merchant. After the death of his mother, his father made a second marriage to a Catholic and decided that he and his children should be baptized. The young Emmanuele showed promise as a scholar, and by the time he was fourteen, the Bishop of Cenada (Monsignore Da Ponte) took the boy under his wing and paid all the costs of his education for the priesthood. As was the custom of the time, the disciple was given his benefactor's name. Da Ponte was ordained in 1773 and became a seminary teacher, with a special interest in Latin, Italian, and French literature. In addition to becoming a follower of the Enlightenment, he involved himself in a number of complicated love affairs, took up with a Venetian noblewoman, and secretly fathered a child. In 1776, he sponsored a public debate at the seminary in Treviso which posed the question whether civilization had succeeded in making mankind any happier. For this affront to Church principles, he was forced to take flight—first to Venice, then to Gorizia, and finally to Dresden, where he began his new career as a librettist. In 1782, he went to Vienna with a letter of introduction to Salieri and was eventually hired as "poeta dei teatri imperiali," a position he held for almost ten years. It was during this period that he met Mozart and collaborated on the three operas that have preserved his name from oblivion. In 1790, however, when Leopold II curbed musical activities in Vienna because of the Turkish war, Da Ponte found himself out of a job. He went to Trieste and fell in love with an English woman named Nancy Grahl or Krahl (the name is still disputed). From there the two of them went to Paris, and then on to London, where they remained for thirteen years. Da Ponte's musical work was restricted to writing a few libretti for undistinguished composers. In 1805, he and Nancy emigrated to America, where he lived out the last thirty-three years of his life, for a time working as a shopkeeper in New Jersey and Pennsylvania, and dying at the age of eighty-nine—one of the first Italians to be buried in the New World. Little by little, everything had changed for him. From the dapper, unctuous ladies' man of his youth, an opportunist steeped in the political intrigues of both Church and court, he became a perfectly ordinary citizen of New York, which in 1805 must have looked like the end of the world to him. From all that to this: a hard-working professor, a dutiful husband, the father of four. When one of his children died, it is said, he was so distraught with grief that he refused to leave his house for almost a year. The point being that, in the end, each life is irreducible to anything other than itself. Which is as much as to say: lives make no sense.

I don't mean to harp on any of this. But the circumstances under which lives shift course are so various that it would seem impossible to say anything about a man until he is dead. Not only is death the one true arbiter of happiness (Solon's remark), it is the only measurement by which we can judge life itself. I once knew a bum who spoke like a Shakespearean actor, a battered, middle-aged alcoholic with scabs on his face and rags for clothes, who slept on the street and begged money from me constantly. Yet he had once been the owner of an art gallery on Madison Avenue. There was another man I knew who had once been considered the most promising young novelist in America. At the time I met him, he had just inherited fifteen thousand dollars from his father and was standing on a New York street corner passing out hundred dollar bills to strangers. It was all part of a plan to destroy the economic system of the United States, he explained to me. Think of what happens. Think of how lives burst apart. Goffe and Whalley, for example, two of the judges who condemned Charles I to death, came to Connecticut after the Restoration and spent the rest of their lives in a cave. Or Mrs. Winchester, the widow of the rifle manufacturer, who feared that the ghosts of the people killed by her husband's rifles were coming to take her soul—and therefore continually added rooms onto her house, creating a monstrous labyrinth of corridors and hideouts, so that she could sleep in a different room every night and thereby elude the ghosts, the irony being that during the San Francisco earthquake of 1906 she was trapped in one of those rooms and nearly starved to death because she couldn't be found by the servants. There is also M. M. Bakhtin, the Russian critic and literary philosopher. During the German invasion of Russia in World War II, he smoked the only copy of one of his manuscripts, a book-length study of German fiction that had taken him years to write. One by one, he took the pages of his manuscript and used the paper to roll his cigarettes, each day smoking a little more of the book until it was gone. These are true stories. They are also parables, perhaps, but they mean what they mean only because they are true.

In his work, Fanshawe shows a particular fondness for stories of this kind. Especially in the notebooks, there is a constant retelling of little anecdotes, and because they are so frequent—and more and more so toward the end—one begins to suspect that Fanshawe felt they could somehow help him to understand himself. One of the very last (from February 1976, just two months before he disappeared) strikes me as significant.

"In a book I once read by Peter Freuchen," Fanshawe writes, "the famous Arctic explorer describes being trapped by a blizzard in northern Greenland. Alone, his supplies dwindling, he decided to build an igloo and wait out the storm. Many days passed. Afraid, above all, that he would be attacked by wolves—for he heard them prowling hungrily on the roof of his igloo—he would periodically step outside and sing at the top of his lungs in order to frighten them away. But the wind was blowing fiercely, and no matter how hard he sang, the only thing he could hear was the wind. If this was a serious problem, however, the problem of the igloo itself was much greater. For Freuchen began to notice that the walls of his little shelter were gradually closing in on him. Because of the particular weather conditions outside, his breath was literally freezing to the walls, and with each breath the walls became that much thicker, the igloo became that much smaller, until eventually there was almost no room left for his body. It is surely a frightening thing, to imagine breathing yourself into a coffin of ice, and to my mind considerably more compelling than, say, *The Pit and the Pendulum* by Poe. For in this case it is the man himself who is the agent of his own destruction, and further, the instrument of that destruction is the very thing he needs to keep himself alive. For surely a man cannot live if he does not breathe. But at the same time, he will not live if he does breathe. Curiously, I do not remember how Freuchen managed to escape his predicament. But needless to say, he did escape. The title of the book, if I recall, is *Arctic Adventure*. It has been out of print for many years."

6

In June of that year (1978), Sophie, Ben, and I went out to New Jersey to see Fanshawe's mother. My parents no longer lived next door (they had retired to Florida), and I had not been back in years. As Ben's grandmother, Mrs. Fanshawe had stayed in touch with us, but relations were somewhat difficult. There seemed to be an undercurrent of hostility in her toward Sophie, as though she secretly blamed her for Fanshawe's disappearance, and this resentment would surface every now and then in some offhand remark. Sophie and I invited her to dinner at reasonable intervals, but she accepted only rarely, and then, when she did come, she would sit there fidgeting and smiling, rattling on in that brittle way of hers, pretending to admire the baby, paying Sophie inappropriate compliments and saying what a lucky girl she was, and then leave early, always getting up in the middle of a conversation and blurting out that she had forgotten an appointment somewhere else. Still, it was hard to hold it against her. Nothing had gone very well in her life, and by now she had more or less stopped hoping it would. Her husband was dead; her daughter had gone through a

long series of mental breakdowns and was now living on
tranquilizers in a halfway house; her son had vanished.
Still beautiful at fifty (as a boy, I thought she was the most
ravishing woman I had ever seen), she kept herself going
with a number of intricate love affairs (the roster of men
was always in flux), shopping sprees in New York, and a
passion for golf. Fanshawe's literary success had taken her
by surprise, but now that she had adjusted to it, she was
perfectly willing to assume responsibility for having given
birth to a genius. When I called to tell her about the
biography, she sounded eager to help. She had letters and
photographs and documents, she said, and would show me
whatever I wanted to see.

We got there by mid-morning, and after an awkward
start, followed by a cup of coffee in the kitchen and a long
talk about the weather, we were taken upstairs to
Fanshawe's old room. Mrs. Fanshawe had prepared quite
thoroughly for me, and all the materials were laid out in
neat piles on what had once been Fanshawe's desk. I was
stunned by the accumulation. Not knowing what to say, I
thanked her for being so helpful—but in fact I was
frightened, overwhelmed by the sheer bulk of what was
there. A few minutes later, Mrs. Fanshawe went downstairs
and out into the backyard with Sophie and Ben (it was a
warm, sunny day), and I was left there alone. I remember
looking out the window and catching a glimpse of Ben as he
waddled across the grass in his diaper-padded overalls,

shrieking and pointing as a robin skimmed overhead. I
tapped on the window, and when Sophie turned around
and looked up, I waved to her. She smiled, blew me a kiss,
and then walked off to inspect a flower bed with Mrs.
Fanshawe.

I settled down behind the desk. It was a terrible thing to
be sitting in that room, and I didn't know how long I would
be able to take it. Fanshawe's baseball glove lay on a shelf
with a scuffed-up baseball inside it; on the shelves above it
and below it were the books he had read as a child; directly
behind me was the bed, with the same blue-and-white
checkered quilt I remembered from years before. This was
the tangible evidence, the remains of a dead world. I had
stepped into the museum of my own past, and what I found
there nearly crushed me.

In one pile: Fanshawe's birth certificate, Fanshawe's
report cards from school, Fanshawe's Cub Scout badges,
Fanshawe's high school diploma. In another pile: photographs. An album of Fanshawe as a baby; an album of
Fanshawe and his sister; an album of the family (Fanshawe
as a two-year-old smiling in his father's arms, Fanshawe
and Ellen hugging their mother on the backyard swing,
Fanshawe surrounded by his cousins). And then the loose
pictures—in folders, in envelopes, in little boxes: dozens of
Fanshawe and me together (swimming, playing catch, riding
bikes, mugging in the yard; my father with the two of us on
his back; the short haircuts, the baggy jeans, the ancient

cars behind us: a Packard, a DeSoto, a wood-panelled Ford station wagon). Class pictures, team pictures, camp pictures. Pictures of races, of games. Sitting in a canoe, pulling on a rope in a tug-of-war. And then, toward the bottom, a few from later years: Fanshawe as I had never seen him. Fanshawe standing in Harvard Yard; Fanshawe on the deck of an Esso oil tanker; Fanshawe in Paris, in front of a stone fountain. Last of all, a single picture of Fanshawe and Sophie—Fanshawe looking older, grimmer; and Sophie so terribly young, so beautiful, and yet somehow distracted, as though unable to concentrate. I took a deep breath and then started to cry, all of a sudden, not aware until the last moment that I had those tears inside me—sobbing hard, shuddering with my face in my hands.

A box to the right of the pictures was filled with letters, at least a hundred of them, beginning at the age of eight (the clumsy writing of a child, smudged pencil marks and erasures) and continuing on through the early seventies. There were letters from college, letters from the ship, letters from France. Most of them were addressed to Ellen, and many were quite long. I knew immediately that they were valuable, no doubt more valuable than anything else in the room—but I didn't have the heart to read them there. I waited ten or fifteen minutes, then went downstairs to join the others.

Mrs. Fanshawe did not want the originals to leave the house, but she had no objection to having the letters photocopied. She even offered to do it herself, but I told her not to bother: I would come out again another day and take care of it.

We had a picnic lunch in the yard. Ben dominated the scene by dashing to the flowers and back again between each bite of his sandwich, and by two o'clock we were ready to go home. Mrs. Fanshawe drove us to the bus station and kissed all three of us goodbye, showing more emotion than at any other time during the visit. Five minutes after the bus started up, Ben fell asleep in my lap, and Sophie took hold of my hand.

"Not such a happy day, was it?" she said.

"One of the worst," I said.

"Imagine having to make conversation with that woman for four hours. I ran out of things to say the moment we got there."

"She probably doesn't like us very much."

"No, I wouldn't think so."

"But that's the least of it."

"It was hard being up there alone, wasn't it?"

"Very hard."

"Any second thoughts?"

"I'm afraid so."

"I don't blame you. The whole thing is getting pretty spooky."

"I'll have to think it through again. Right now, I'm beginning to feel I've made a big mistake."

•

Four days later, Mrs. Fanshawe telephoned to say that she was going to Europe for a month and that perhaps it would be a good idea for us to take care of our business now (her words). I had been planning to let the matter slide, but before I could think of a decent excuse for not going out there, I heard myself agreeing to make the trip the following Monday. Sophie backed off from accompanying me, and I didn't press her to change her mind. We both felt that one family visit had been enough.

Jane Fanshawe met me at the bus station, all smiles and affectionate hellos. From the moment I climbed into her car, I sensed that things were going to be different this time. She had made an effort with her appearance (white pants, a red silk blouse, her tanned, unwrinkled neck exposed), and it was hard not to feel that she was enticing me to look at her, to acknowledge the fact that she was still beautiful. But there was more to it than that: a vaguely insinuating tone to her voice, an assumption that we were somehow old friends, on an intimate footing because of the past, and wasn't it lucky that I had come by myself, since now we were free to talk openly with each other. I found it all rather distasteful and said no more than I had to.

"That's quite a little family you have there, my boy," she said, turning to me as we stopped for a red light.

"Yes," I said. "Quite a little family."

"The baby is adorable, of course. A regular heartthrob. But a bit on the wild side, wouldn't you say?"

"He's only two. Most children tend to be high-spirited at that age."

"Of course. But I do think that Sophie dotes on him. She seems so amused all the time, if you know what I mean. I'm not arguing against laughter, but a little discipline wouldn't hurt either."

"Sophie acts that way with everyone," I said. "A lively woman is bound to be a lively mother. As far as I can tell, Ben has no complaints."

A slight pause, and then, as we started up again, cruising along a broad commercial avenue, Jane Fanshawe added: "She's a lucky girl, that Sophie. Lucky to have landed on her feet. Lucky to have found a man like you."

"I usually think of it the other way around," I said.

"You shouldn't be so modest."

"I'm not. It's just that I know what I'm talking about. So far, all the luck has been on my side."

She smiled at this—briefly, enigmatically, as though judging me a dunce, and yet somehow conceding the point, aware that I wasn't going to give her an opening. By the time we reached her house a few minutes later, she seemed to have dropped her initial tactics. Sophie and Ben were no longer mentioned, and she became a model of solicitude, telling me how glad she was that I was writing the book about Fanshawe, acting as though her encouragement made a real difference—an ultimate sort of approval, not only of the book but of who I was. Then, handing me the keys to her car, she told me how to get to the nearest photocopy store. Lunch, she said, would be waiting for me when I got back.

It took more than two hours to copy the letters, which made it nearly one o'clock by the time I returned to the house. Lunch was indeed there, and it was an impressive spread: asparagus, cold salmon, cheeses, white wine, the works. It was all set out on the dining room table, accompanied by flowers and what were clearly the best dishes. The surprise must have shown on my face.

"I wanted to make it festive." Mrs. Fanshawe said. "You have no idea how good it makes me feel to have you here. All the memories that come back. It's as though the bad things never happened."

I suspected that she had already started drinking while I was gone. Still in control, still steady in her movements, there was a certain thickening that had crept into her voice, a wavering, effusive quality that had not been there before. As we sat down to the table, I told myself to watch it. The wine was poured in liberal doses, and when I saw her paying more attention to her glass than to her plate, merely picking at her food and eventually ignoring it altogether, I began to expect the worst. After some idle talk about my parents and my two younger sisters, the conversation lapsed into a monologue.

"It's strange," she said, "strange how things in life turn out. From one moment to the next, you never know what's going to happen. Here you are, the little boy who lived next door. You're the same person who used to run through this house with mud on his shoes—all grown up now, a man. You're the father of my grandson, do you realize that? You're married to my son's wife. If someone had told me ten years ago that this was the future, I would have laughed. That's what you finally learn from life: how strange it is. You can't keep up with what happens. You can't even imagine it.

"You even look like him, you know. You always did, the two of you—like brothers, almost like twins. I remember how when you were both small I would sometimes confuse you from a distance. I couldn't even tell which one of you was mine.

"I know how much you loved him, how you looked up to him. But let me tell you something, my dear. He wasn't half the boy you were. He was cold inside. He was all dead in there, and I don't think he ever loved anyone—not once, not ever in his life. I'd sometimes watch you and your mother across the yard—the way you would run to her and throw your arms around her neck, the way you would let her kiss you—and right there, smack in front of me, I could see everything I didn't have with my own son. He wouldn't let me touch him, you know. After the age of four or five, he'd cringe every time I got near him. How do you think that makes a woman feel—to have her own son despise her? I was so damned young back then. I wasn't even twenty when he was born. Imagine what it does to you to be rejected like that.

"I'm not saying that he was bad. He was a separate being, a child without parents. Nothing I said ever had an effect on him. The same with his father. He refused to learn anything from us. Robert tried and tried, but he could never get through to the boy. But you can't punish someone for a lack of affection, can you? You can't force a child to love you just because he's your child.

"There was Ellen, of course. Poor, tortured Ellen. He was good to her, we both know that. But too good somehow, and in the end it wasn't good for her at all. He brainwashed her. He made her so dependent on him that she began to think twice before turning to us. He was the one who understood her, the one who gave her advice, the one who could solve her problems. Robert and I were no more than figureheads. As far as the children were concerned, we hardly existed. Ellen trusted her brother so much that she finally gave up her soul to him. I'm not saying that he knew what he was doing, but I still have to live with the results. The girl is twenty-seven years old, but she acts as though she were fourteen—and that's when she's doing well. She's so confused, so panicked inside herself. One day she thinks I'm out to destroy her, the next day she calls me thirty times on the telephone. Thirty times. You can't even begin to imagine what it's like.

"Ellen's the reason why he never published any of his

work, you know. She's why he quit Harvard after his second year. He was writing poetry back then, and every few weeks he would send her a batch of manuscripts. You know what those poems are like. They're almost impossible to understand. Very passionate, of course, filled with all that ranting and exhortation, but so obscure you'd think they were written in code. Ellen would spend hours puzzling over them, acting as if her life depended on it, treating the poems as secret messages, oracles written directly to her. I don't think he had any idea what was happening. Her brother was gone, you see, and these poems were all she had left of him. The poor baby. She was only fifteen at the time, and already falling to pieces anyway. She would pore over those pages until they were all crumpled and dirty, lugging them around with her wherever she went. When she got really bad, she would go up to perfect strangers on the bus and force them into their hands. 'Read these poems,' she'd say. 'They'll save your life.'

"Eventually, of course, she had that first breakdown. She wandered off from me in the supermarket one day, and before I knew it she was taking those big jugs of apple juice off the shelves and smashing them on the floor. One after another, like someone in a trance, standing in all that broken glass, her ankles bleeding, the juice running everywhere. It was horrible. She got so wild, it took three men to restrain her and carry her off.

"I'm not saying that her brother was responsible. But

those damned poems certainly didn't help, and rightly or wrongly he blamed himself. From then on, he never tried to publish anything. He came to visit Ellen in the hospital, and I think it was too much for him, seeing her like that, totally beside herself, totally crazy—screaming at him and accusing him of hating her. It was a real schizoid break, you know, and he wasn't able to deal with it. That's when he took the vow not to publish. It was a kind of penance, I think, and he stuck to it for the rest of his life, didn't he, he stuck to it in that stubborn, brutal way of his, right to the end.

"About two months later, I got a letter from him informing me that he had quit college. He wasn't asking my advice, mind you, he was telling me what he'd done. Dear mother, and so on and so forth, all very noble and impressive. I'm dropping out of school to relieve you of the financial burden of supporting me. What with Ellen's condition, the huge medical costs, the blankety x and y and z, and so on and so forth.

"I was furious. A boy like that throwing his education away for nothing. It was an act of sabotage, but there wasn't anything I could do about it. He was already gone. A friend of his at Harvard had a father who had some connection with shipping—I think he represented the seamen's union or something—and he managed to get his papers through that man. By the time the letter reached me, he was in Texas somewhere, and that was that. I didn't see him again for more than five years.

"Every month or so a letter or postcard would come for Ellen, but there was never any return address. Paris, the south of France, God knows where, but he made sure that we didn't have any way of getting in touch with him. I found this behavior despicable. Cowardly and despicable. Don't ask me why I saved the letters. I'm sorry I didn't burn them. That's what I should have done. Burned the whole lot of them."

She went on like this for more than an hour, her words gradually mounting in bitterness, at some point reaching a moment of sustained clarity, and then, following the next glass of wine, gradually losing coherence. Her voice was hypnotic. As long as she went on speaking, I felt that nothing could touch me anymore. There was a sense of being immune, of being protected by the words that came from her mouth. I scarcely bothered to listen. I was floating inside that voice, I was surrounded by it, buoyed up by its persistence, going with the flow of syllables, the rise and fall, the waves. As the afternoon light came streaming through the windows onto the table, sparkling in the sauces, the melting butter, the green wine bottles, everything in the room became so radiant and still that I began to find it unreal that I should be sitting there in my own body. I'm melting, I said to myself, watching the butter soften in its dish, and once or twice I even thought that I mustn't let this go on, that I mustn't allow the moment to slip away from me, but in the end I did nothing about it, feeling somehow that I couldn't.

I make no excuses for what happened. Drunkenness is never more than a symptom, not an absolute cause, and I realize that it would be wrong of me to try to defend myself. Nevertheless, there is at least the possibility of an explanation. I am fairly certain now that the things that followed had as much to do with the past as with the present, and I find it odd, now that I have some distance from it, to see how a number of ancient feelings finally caught up with me that afternoon. As I sat there listening to Mrs. Fanshawe, it was hard not to remember how I had seen her as a boy, and once this began to happen, I found myself stumbling onto images that had not been visible to me in years. There was one in particular that struck me with great force: an afternoon in August when I was thirteen or fourteen, looking through my bedroom window into the yard next door and seeing Mrs. Fanshawe walk out in a red two-piece bathing suit, casually unhook the top half, and lie down on a lawn chair with her back to the sun. All this happened by chance. I had been sitting by my window day-dreaming, and then, unexpectedly, a beautiful woman comes sauntering into my field of vision, almost naked, unaware of my presence, as though I had conjured her myself. This image stayed with me for a long time, and I returned to it often during my adolescence: a little boy's lust, the quick of late-night fantasies. Now that this woman was apparently in the act of seducing me, I hardly knew what to think. On the one hand, I found the scene grotesque. On the other hand, there was something natural about it, even logical, and I sensed that if I didn't use all my strength to fight it, I was going to allow it to happen.

There's no question that she made me pity her. Her version of Fanshawe was so anguished, so fraught with the signs of genuine unhappiness, that I gradually weakened to her, fell into her trap. What I still don't understand, however, is to what extent she was conscious of what she was doing. Had she planned it in advance, or did the thing just happen by itself? Was her rambling speech a ploy to wear down my resistance, or was it a spontaneous burst of true feeling? I suspect that she was telling the truth about Fanshawe, her own truth at any rate, but that is not enough to convince me—for even a child knows that the truth can be used for devious ends. More importantly, there is the question of motive. Close to six years after the fact, I still haven't come up with an answer. To say that she found me irresistible would be far-fetched, and I am not willing to delude myself about that. It was much deeper, much more sinister. Recently, I've begun to wonder if she didn't somehow sense a hatred in me for Fanshawe that was just as strong as her own. Perhaps she felt this unspoken bond between us, perhaps it was the kind of bond that could be proved only through some perverse, extravagant act. Fucking me would be like fucking Fanshawe—like fucking her own son—and in the darkness of this sin, she would have him again—but only in order to destroy him. A terrible revenge. If this is true, then I do not have the luxury of calling myself her victim. If anything, I was her accomplice.

It began not long after she started to cry—when she finally exhausted herself and the words broke apart, crumbling into tears. Drunk, filled with emotion, I stood up, walked over to where she was sitting, and put my arms around her in a gesture of comfort. This carried us across the threshold. Mere contact was enough to trigger a sexual response, a blind memory of other bodies, of other embraces, and a moment later we were kissing, and then, not many moments after that, lying naked on her bed upstairs.

Although I was drunk, I was not so far gone that I didn't know what I was doing. But not even guilt was enough to stop me. This moment will end, I said to myself, and no one will be hurt. It has nothing to do with my life, nothing to do with Sophie. But then, even as it was happening, I discovered there was more to it than that. For the fact was that I liked fucking Fanshawe's mother—but in a way that had nothing to do with pleasure. I was consumed, and for the first time in my life I found no tenderness inside me. I was fucking out of hatred, and I turned it into an act of violence, grinding away at this woman as though I wanted to pulverize her. I had entered my own darkness, and it was there that I learned the one thing that is more terrible than anything else: that sexual desire can also be the desire to kill, that a moment comes when it is possible for a man to choose death over life. This woman wanted me to hurt her, and I did, and I found myself revelling in my cruelty. But even then I knew that I was only halfway home, that she was no more than a shadow, and that I was using her to attack Fanshawe himself. As I came into her the second time—the two of us covered with sweat, groaning like creatures in a nightmare—I finally understood this. I wanted to kill Fanshawe. I wanted Fanshawe to be dead, and I was going to do it. I was going to track him down and kill him.

I left her in the bed asleep, crept out of the room, and called for a taxi from the phone downstairs. Half an hour later I was on the bus back to New York. At the Port Authority Terminal, I went into the men's room and washed my hands and face, then took the subway uptown. I got home just as Sophie was setting the table for dinner.

7

The worst of it began then. There were so many things to hide from Sophie, I could barely show myself to her at all. I turned edgy, remote, shut myself up in my little work-room, craved only solitude. For a long time Sophie bore with me, acting with a patience I had no right to expect, but in the end even she began to wear out, and by the middle of the summer we had started quarreling, picking at each other, squabbling over things that meant nothing. One day I walked into the house and found her crying on the bed, and I knew then that I was on the verge of smashing my life.

For Sophie, the problem was the book. If only I would stop working on it, then things would return to normal. I had been too hasty, she said. The project was a mistake, and I should not be stubborn about admitting it. She was right, of course, but I kept arguing the other side to her: I had committed myself to the book, I had signed a contract for it, and it would be cowardly to back out. What I didn't tell her was that I no longer had any intention of writing it. The book existed for me now only in so far as it could lead me to Fanshawe, and beyond that there was no book at all.

It had become a private matter for me, something no longer connected to writing. All the research for the biography, all the facts I would uncover as I dug into his past, all the work that seemed to belong to the book—these were the very things I would use to find out where he was. Poor Sophie. She never had the slightest notion of what I was up to—for what I claimed to be doing was in fact no different from what I actually did. I was piecing together the story of a man's life. I was gathering information, collecting names, places, dates, establishing a chronology of events. Why I persisted like this still baffles me. Everything had been reduced to a single impulse: to find Fanshawe, to speak to Fanshawe, to confront Fanshawe one last time. But I could never take it farther than that, could never pin down an image of what I was hoping to achieve by such an encounter. Fanshawe had written that he would kill me, but that threat did not scare me off. I knew that I had to find him— that nothing would be settled until I did. This was the given, the first principle, the mystery of faith: I acknowledged it, but I did not bother to question it.

In the end, I don't think that I really intended to kill him. The murderous vision that had come to me with Mrs. Fanshawe did not last, at least not on any conscious level. There were times when little scenes would flash through my head—of strangling Fanshawe, of stabbing him, of shooting him in the heart—but others had died similar deaths inside me over the years, and I did not pay much attention to them. The strange thing was not that I might have wanted to kill Fanshawe, but that I sometimes imagined he *wanted* me to kill him. This happened only once or twice—at moments of extreme lucidity—and I became convinced that this was the true meaning of the letter he had written. Fanshawe was waiting for me. He had chosen me as his executioner, and he knew that he could trust me to carry out the job. But that was precisely why I wasn't going to do it. Fanshawe's power had to be broken, not submitted to. The point was to prove to him that I no longer cared—that was the crux of it: to treat him as a dead man, even though he was alive. But before I proved this to Fanshawe, I had to prove it to myself, and the fact that I needed to prove it was proof that I still cared too much. It was not enough for me to let things take their course. I had to shake them up, bring them to a head. Because I still doubted myself, I needed to run risks, to test myself before the greatest possible danger. Killing Fanshawe would mean nothing. The point was to find him alive—and then to walk away from him alive.

The letters to Ellen were useful. Unlike the notebooks, which tended to be speculative and devoid of detail, the letters were highly specific. I sensed that Fanshawe was making an effort to entertain his sister, to cheer her up with amusing stories, and consequently the references were more personal than elsewhere. Names, for example, were often mentioned—of college friends, of shipmates, of people he knew in France. And if there were no return addresses on the envelopes, there were nevertheless many places discussed: Baytown, Corpus Christi, Charleston, Baton Rouge, Tampa, different neighborhoods in Paris, a village in southern France. These things were enough to get me started, and for several weeks I sat in my room making lists, correlating people with places, places with times, times with people, drawing maps and calendars, looking up addresses, writing letters. I was hunting for leads, and anything that held even the slightest promise I tried to pursue. My assumption was that somewhere along the line Fanshawe had made a mistake—that someone knew where he was, that someone from the past had seen him. This was by no means sure, but it seemed like the only plausible way to begin.

The college letters are rather plodding and sincere— accounts of books read, discussions with friends, descriptions of dormitory life—but these come from the period before Ellen's breakdown, and they have an intimate, confidential tone that the future letters abandon. On the ship, for example, Fanshawe rarely says anything about himself—except as it might pertain to an anecdote he has chosen to tell. We see him trying to fit into his new surroundings, playing cards in the dayroom with an oiler from Louisiana (and winning), playing pool in various low-life bars ashore (and winning), and then explaining his

success as a fluke: "I'm so geared up not to fall on my face,
I've somehow gone beyond myself. A surge of adrenalin, I
think." Descriptions of working overtime in the engine
room, "a hundred and forty degrees, if you can believe it—
my sneakers filled up with so much sweat, they squished as
though I'd been walking in puddles"; of having a wisdom
tooth pulled by a drunken dentist in Baytown, Texas,
"blood all over the place, and little bits of tooth cluttering
the hole in my gums for a week." As a newcomer with no
seniority, Fanshawe was moved from job to job. At each
port there were crew members who left the ship to go home
and others who came aboard to take their places, and if one
of these fresh arrivals preferred Fanshawe's job to the one
that was open, the Kid (as he was called) would be bumped
to something else. Fanshawe therefore worked variously as
an ordinary seaman (scraping and painting the deck), as a
utility man (mopping floors, making beds, cleaning toilets),
and as a messman (serving food and washing dishes). This
last job was the hardest, but it was also the most interesting,
since ship life chiefly revolves around the subject of food:
the great appetites nurtured by boredom, the men literally
living from one meal to the next, the surprising delicacy of
some of them (fat, coarse men judging dishes with the
haughtiness and disdain of eighteenth-century French
dukes). But Fanshawe was given good advice by an old-
timer the day he started the job: "Don't take no shit from
no one," the man said. "If a guy complains about the food,

tell him to button it. If he keeps it up, act like he's not there
and serve him last. If that don't do the trick, tell him you'll
put ice water in his soup the next time. Even better, tell him
you'll piss in it. You gotta let them know who's boss."

We see Fanshawe carrying the captain his breakfast one
morning after a night of violent storms off Cape Hatteras:
Fanshawe putting the grapefruit, the scrambled eggs, and
the toast on a tray, wrapping the tray in tinfoil, then
further wrapping it in towels, hoping the plates will not
blow off into the water when he reaches the bridge (since
the wind is holding at seventy miles per hour); Fanshawe
then climbing up the ladder, taking his first steps on the
bridge, and then, suddenly, as the wind hits him, doing a
wild pirouette—the ferocious air shooting under the tray
and pulling his arms up over his head, as though he were
holding on to a primitive flying machine, about to launch
himself over the water; Fanshawe, summoning all his
strength to pull down the tray, finally wrestling it to a
position flat against his chest, the plates miraculously not
slipping, and then, step by struggling step, walking the
length of the bridge, a tiny figure dwarfed by the havoc of
the air around him; Fanshawe, after how many minutes,
making it to the other end, entering the forecastle, finding
the plump captain behind the wheel, saying, "Your breakfast, captain," and the helmsman turning, giving him the
briefest glance of recognition and replying, in a distracted
voice, "Thanks, kid. Just put it on the table over there."

Not everything was so amusing to Fanshawe, however. There is mention of a fight (no details given) that seems to have disturbed him, along with several ugly scenes he witnessed ashore. An instance of nigger-baiting in a Tampa bar, for example: a crowd of drunks ganging up on an old black man who had wandered in with a large American flag—wanting to sell it—and the first drunk opening the flag and saying there weren't enough stars on it—"this flag's a fake"—and the old man denying it, almost grovelling for mercy, as the other drunks start grumbling in support of the first—the whole thing ending when the old man is pushed out the door, landing flat on the sidewalk, and the drunks nodding approval, dismissing the matter with a few comments about making the world safe for democracy. "I felt humiliated," Fanshawe wrote, "ashamed of myself for being there."

Still, the letters are basically jocular in tone ("Call me Redburn," one of them begins), and by the end one senses that Fanshawe has managed to prove something to himself. The ship is no more than an excuse, an arbitrary otherness, a way to test himself against the unknown. As with any initiation, survival itself is the triumph. What begin as possible liabilities—his Harvard education, his middle-class background—he eventually turns to his advantage, and by the end of his stint he is the acknowledged intellectual of the crew, no longer just the "Kid" but at times also the "Professor," brought in to arbitrate disputes (who was the twenty-third President, what is the population of Florida, who played left field for the 1947 Giants) and consulted regularly as a source of obscure information. Crew members ask his help in filling out bureaucratic forms (tax schedules, insurance questionnaires, accident reports), and some even ask him to write letters for them (in one case, seventeen love letters for Otis Smart to his girlfriend Sue-Ann in Dido, Louisiana). The point is not that Fanshawe becomes the center of attention, but that he manages to fit in, to find a place for himself. The true test, after all, is to be like everyone else. Once that happens, he no longer has to question his singularity. He is free—not only of others, but of himself. The ultimate proof of this, I think, is that when he leaves the ship, he says goodbye to no one. He signs off one night in Charleston, collects his pay from the captain, and then just disappears. Two weeks later he arrives in Paris.

No word for two months. And then, for the next three months, nothing but postcards. Brief, elliptical messages scrawled on the back of commonplace tourist shots: Sacré Coeur, the Eiffel Tower, the Conciergerie. When the letters do begin to come, they arrive fitfully, and say nothing of any great importance. We know that by now Fanshawe is deep into his work (numerous early poems, a first draft of *Blackouts*), but the letters give no real sense of the life he is leading. One feels that he is in conflict, unsure of himself in regard to Ellen, not wanting to lose touch with her and yet unable to decide how much or how little to tell her. (And the fact is that most of these letters are not even read by Ellen. Addressed to the house in New Jersey, they are of course opened by Mrs. Fanshawe, who screens them before showing them to her daughter—and more often than not, Ellen does not see them. Fanshawe, I think, must have known this would happen, at least would have suspected it. Which further complicates the matter—since in some way these letters are not written to Ellen at all. Ellen, finally, is no more than a literary device, the medium through which Fanshawe communicates with his mother. Hence her anger. For even as he speaks to her, he can pretend to ignore her.)

For about a year the letters dwell almost exclusively on objects (buildings, streets, descriptions of Paris), hashing out meticulous catalogues of things seen and heard, but Fanshawe himself is barely present. Then, gradually, we begin to see some of his acquaintances, to sense a slow gravitation towards the anecdote—but still, the stories are divorced from any context, which gives them a floating, disembodied quality. We see, for example, an old Russian composer by the name of Ivan Wyshnegradsky, now nearly eighty years old—impoverished, a widower, living alone in a shabby apartment on the rue Mademoiselle. "I see this man more than anyone else," Fanshawe declares. Then not a word about their friendship, not a glimmer of what they say to each other. Instead, there is a lengthy description of the quarter-tone piano in the apartment, with its enormous

bulk and multiple keyboards (built for Wyshnegradsky in
Prague almost fifty years before, and one of only three
quarter-tone pianos in Europe), and then, making no
further allusions to the composer's career, the story of how
Fanshawe gives the old man a refrigerator. "I was moving
to another apartment last month," Fanshawe writes.
"Since the place was furnished with a new refrigerator, I
decided to give the old one to Ivan as a present. Like many
people in Paris, he has never had a refrigerator—storing
his food for all these years in a little box in the wall of his
kitchen. He seemed quite pleased by the offer, and I made
all the arrangements to have it delivered to his house—
carrying it upstairs with the help of the man who drove the
truck. Ivan greeted the arrival of this machine as an
important event in his life—bubbling over like a small
child—and yet he was wary, I could see that, even a bit
daunted, not quite sure what to make of this alien object.
'It's so big,' he kept saying, as we worked it into place, and
then, when we plugged it in and the motor started up—
'Such a lot of noise.' I assured him that he would get used
to it, pointing out all the advantages of this modern
convenience, all the ways in which his life would be
improved. I felt like a missionary: big Father Know-It-All,
redeeming the life of this stone-age man by showing him the
true religion. A week or so went by, and Ivan called me
nearly every day to tell me how happy he was with the
refrigerator, describing all the new foods he was able to

buy and keep in his house. Then disaster. 'I think it's
broken,' he said to me one day, sounding very contrite.
The little freezer section on top had apparently filled up
with frost, and not knowing how to get rid of it, he had
used a hammer, banging away not only at the ice but at the
coils below it. 'My dear friend,' he said, 'I'm very sorry.' I
told him not to fret—I would find a repairman to fix it. A
long pause on the other end. 'Well,' he said at last, 'I think
maybe it's better this way. The noise, you know. It makes
it very hard to concentrate. I've lived so long with my little
box in the wall, I feel rather attached to it. My dear friend,
don't be angry. I'm afraid there's nothing to be done with
an old man like me. You get to a certain point in life, and
then it's too late to change.' "

Further letters continue this trend, with various names
mentioned, various jobs alluded to. I gather that the money
Fanshawe earned on the ship lasted for about a year and
that afterwards he scrambled as best he could. For a time
it seems that he translated a series of art books; at another
time there is evidence that he worked as an English tutor
for several lycée students; still again, it seems that he
worked the graveyard shift one summer at the *New York
Times* Paris office as a switchboard operator (which, if
nothing else, indicates that he had become fluent in
French); and then there is a rather curious period during
which he worked off and on for a movie producer—revising
treatments, translating, preparing script synopses. Al-

though there are few autobiographical allusions in any of Fanshawe's works, I believe that certain incidents in *Neverland* can be traced back to this last experience (Montag's house in chapter seven; Flood's dream in chapter thirty). "The strange thing about this man," Fanshawe writes (referring to the movie producer in one of his letters), "is that while his financial dealings with the rich border on the criminal (cutthroat tactics, outright lying), he is quite gentle with those down on their luck. People who owe him money are rarely sued or taken to court—but are given a chance to work off their debts by rendering him services. His chauffeur, for example, is a destitute marquis who drives around in a white Mercedes. There is an old baron who does nothing but xerox papers. Every time I visit the apartment to turn in my work, there is some new lackey standing in the corner, some decrepit nobleman hiding behind the curtains, some elegant financier who turns out to be the messenger boy. Nor does anything go to waste. When the ex-director who had been living in the maid's room on the sixth floor committed suicide last month, I inherited his overcoat—and have been wearing it ever since. A long black affair that comes down almost to my ankles. It makes me look like a spy."

As for Fanshawe's private life, there are only the vaguest hints. A dinner party is referred to, a painter's studio is described, the name Anne sneaks out once or twice—but the nature of these connections is obscure. This was the kind of thing I needed, however. By doing the necessary legwork, by going out and asking enough questions, I figured I would eventually be able to track some of these people down.

Besides a three-week trip to Ireland (Dublin, Cork, Limerick, Sligo), Fanshawe seems to have remained more or less fixed. The final draft of *Blackouts* was completed at some point during his second year in Paris; *Miracles* was written during the third, along with forty or fifty short poems. All this is rather easy to determine—since it was around this time that Fanshawe developed the habit of dating his work. Still unclear is the precise moment when he left Paris for the country, but I believe it falls somewhere between June and September of 1971. The letters become sparse just then, and even the notebooks give no more than a list of the books he was reading (Raleigh's *History of the World* and *The Journeys* of Cabeza de Vaca). But once he is ensconced in the country house, he gives a fairly elaborate account of how he wound up there. The details are unimportant in themselves, but one crucial thing emerges: while living in France Fanshawe did not hide the fact that he was a writer. His friends knew about his work, and if there was ever any secret, it was only meant for his family. This is a definite slip on his part—the only time in any of the letters he gives himself away. "The Dedmons, an American couple I know in Paris," he writes, "are unable to visit their country house for the next year (they're going to Japan). Since the place has been broken into once or twice, they're reluctant to leave it empty—and have offered me the job of caretaker. Not only do I get it rent-free, but I'm also given the use of a car and a small salary (enough to get by on if I'm very careful). This is a lucky break. They said they would much rather pay me to sit in the house and write for a year than rent it out to strangers." A small point, perhaps, but when I came across it in the letter, I was heartened. Fanshawe had momentarily let down his guard—and if it happened once, there was no reason to assume it could not happen again.

As examples of writing, the letters from the country surpass all the others. By now, Fanshawe's eye has become incredibly sharp, and one senses a new availability of words inside him, as though the distance between seeing and writing had been narrowed, the two acts now almost identical, part of a single, unbroken gesture. Fanshawe is preoccupied by the landscape, and he keeps returning to it, endlessly watching it, endlessly recording its changes. His patience before these things is never less than remarkable, and there are passages of nature writing in both the letters and notebooks as luminous as any I have read. The stone house he lives in (walls two feet thick) was built during the Revolution: on one side is a small vineyard, on the other side is a meadow where sheep graze; there is a forest behind (magpies, rooks, wild boar), and in front, across the road, are the cliffs that lead up to the village (population forty). On these same cliffs, hidden in a tangle of bushes and trees, are the ruins of a chapel that once belonged to the Knights Templars. Broom, thyme, scrub oak, red soil, white clay, the Mistral—Fanshawe lives amidst these things for more than a year, and little by little they seem to alter him, to ground him more deeply in himself. I hesitate to talk about a religious or mystical experience (these terms mean nothing to me), but from all the evidence it seems that Fanshawe was alone for the whole time, barely seeing anyone, barely even opening his mouth. The stringency of this life disciplined him. Solitude became a passageway into the self, an instrument of discovery. Although he was still quite young at the time, I believe this period marked the beginning of his maturity as a writer. From now on, the work is no longer promising— it is fulfilled, accomplished, unmistakably his own. Starting with the long sequence of poems written in the country (*Ground Work*), and then on through the plays and *Neverland* (all written in New York), Fanshawe is in full flower. One looks for traces of madness, for signs of the thinking that eventually turned him against himself— but the work reveals nothing of the sort. Fanshawe is no doubt an unusual person, but to all appearances he is sane, and when he returns to America in the fall of 1972, he seems totally in command of himself.

My first answers came from the people Fanshawe had

known at Harvard. The word *biography* seemed to open doors for me, and I had no trouble getting appointments to see most of them. I saw his freshman roommate; I saw several of his friends; I saw two or three of the Radcliffe girls he had dated. Nothing much came of it, however. Of all the people I met, only one said anything of interest. This was Paul Schiff, whose father had made the arrangements for Fanshawe's job on the oil tanker. Schiff was now a pediatrician in Westchester County, and we spoke in his office one evening until quite late. There was an earnestness about him that I liked (a small, intense man, his hair already thinning, with steady eyes and a soft, resonant voice), and he talked openly, without any prodding. Fanshawe had been an important person in his life, and he remembered their friendship well. "I was a diligent boy," Schiff said. "Hard-working, obedient, without much imag- ination. Fanshawe wasn't intimidated by Harvard the way the rest of us were, and I think I was in awe of that. He had read more than anyone else—more poets, more philoso- phers, more novelists—but the business of school seemed to bore him. He didn't care about grades, cut class a lot, just seemed to go his own way. In freshman year, we lived down the hall from each other, and for some reason he picked me out to be his friend. After that, I sort of tagged along after him. Fanshawe had so many ideas about everything, I think I learned more from him than from any of my classes. It was a bad case of hero-worship, I suppose—but Fanshawe helped me, and I haven't forgotten it. He was the one who taught me to think for myself, to make my own choices. If it hadn't been for him, I never would have become a doctor. I switched to premed because he convinced me to do what I wanted to do, and I'm still grateful to him for it.

"Midway through our second year, Fanshawe told me that he was going to quit school. It didn't really surprise me. Cambridge wasn't the right place for Fanshawe, and I knew that he was restless, itching to get away. I talked to my father, who represented the seamen's union, and he worked out that job for Fanshawe on the ship. It was arranged very neatly. Fanshawe was whisked through all the paperwork, and a few weeks later he was off. I heard from him several times—postcards from here and there. Hi, how are you, that kind of thing. It didn't bother me though, and I was glad that I'd been able to do something for him. But then, all those good feelings eventually blew up in my face. I was in the city one day about four years ago, walking along Fifth Avenue, and I ran into Fanshawe, right there on the street. I was delighted to see him, really surprised and happy, but he hardly even talked to me. It was as though he'd forgotten who I was. Very stiff, almost rude. I had to force my address and phone number into his hand. He promised to call, but of course he never did. It hurt a lot, I can tell you. The son-of-a-bitch, I thought to myself, who does he think he is? He wouldn't even tell me what he was doing—just evaded my questions and sauntered off. So much for college days, I thought. So much for friendship. It left an ugly taste in my mouth. Last year, my wife bought one of his books and gave it to me as a birthday present. I know it's childish, but I haven't had the heart to open it. It just sits there on the shelf collecting dust. It's very strange, isn't it? Everyone says it's a masterpiece, but I don't think I can ever bring myself to read it."

This was the most lucid commentary I got from anyone. Some of the oil tanker shipmates had things to say, but nothing that really served my purpose. Otis Smart, for example, remembered the love letters Fanshawe had written for him. When I reached him by telephone in Baton Rouge, he went on about them at great length, even quoting some of the phrases Fanshawe had made up ("my darling twinkle-toes," "my pumpkin squash woman," "my wallow-dream wickedness," and so on), laughing as he spoke. The damndest thing was, he said, that the whole time he was sending those letters to Sue-Ann, she was fooling around with someone else, and the day he got home she announced to him that she was getting married. "It's just as well," Smart added. "I ran into Sue-Ann back home last year, and she's up to about three hundred pounds now. She looks like a cartoon fat lady—strutting down the street in orange stretch pants with a mess of brats bawling around her. It made me laugh, it did—remembering the letters. That Fanshawe really cracked me up. He'd get going with some of those lines of his, and I'd start rolling on the floor like a monkey. It's too bad about what happened. You hate to hear about a guy punching his ticket so young."

Jeffrey Brown, now a chef in a Houston restaurant, had been the assistant cook on the ship. He remembered Fanshawe as the one white crew member who had been friendly to him. "It wasn't easy," Brown said. "The crew was mostly a bunch of rednecks, and they'd just as soon spit at me as say hello. But Fanshawe stuck by me, didn't care what anyone thought. When we got into Baytown and places like that, we'd go ashore together for drinks, for girls, whatever. I knew those towns better than Fanshawe did, and I told him that if he wanted to stick with me, we couldn't go into the regular sailors' bars. I knew what my ass would be worth in places like that, and I didn't want trouble. No problem, Fanshawe said, and off we'd go to the black sections, no problem at all. Most of the time, things were pretty calm on the ship—nothing I couldn't handle. But then this rough customer came on for a few weeks. A guy named Cutbirth, if you can believe it, Roy Cutbirth. He was a stupid honky oiler who finally got thrown off the ship when the Chief Engineer figured out he didn't know squat about engines. He'd cheated on his oiler's test to get the job—just the man to have down there if you want to blow up the ship. This Cutbirth was dumb, mean and dumb. He had those tattoos on his knuckles—a letter on each finger: L-O-V-E on the right hand, H-A-T-E on the left. When you see that kind of crazy shit, you just want to keep away. This guy once bragged to Fanshawe about how he used to spend his Saturday nights back home in Alabama—sitting on a hill over the interstate and shooting at cars. A charming fellow, no matter how you put it. And then there was this sick eye he had, all bloodshot and messed up. But he liked to brag about that, too. Seems he got it one day when a piece of glass flew into it. That was in Selma, he said, throwing bottles at Martin Luther King. I don't have to tell you that this Cutbirth wasn't my bosom buddy. He used to give me a lot of stares, muttering under his breath and nodding to himself, but I paid no attention. Things went on like that for a while. Then he tried it with Fanshawe around, and the way it came out, it was just a little too loud for Fanshawe to ignore. He stops, turns to Cutbirth, and says, 'What did you say?' And Cutbirth, all tough and cocky, says something like 'I was just wondering when you and the jungle bunny are getting married, sweetheart.' Well, Fanshawe was always peaceable and friendly, a real gentleman, if you know what I mean, and so I wasn't expecting what happened. It was like watching that hulk on the t.v., the man who turns into a beast. All of a sudden he got angry, I mean raging, damned near *beside* himself with anger. He grabbed Cutbirth by the shirt and just threw him against the wall, just pinned him there and held on, breathing right into his face. 'Don't ever say that again,' Fanshawe says, his eyes all on fire. 'Don't ever say that again, or I'll kill you.' And damned if you didn't believe him when he said it. The guy was ready to kill, and Cutbirth knew it. 'Just joking,' he says. 'Just making a little joke.' And that was the end of it— real fast. The whole thing didn't take more than half a blink. About two days later, Cutbirth got fired. A lucky thing, too. If he'd stayed around any longer, there's no telling what might have happened."

I got dozens of statements like this one—from letters, from phone conversations, from interviews. It went on for months, and each day the material expanded, grew in geometric surges, accumulating more and more associations, a chain of contacts that eventually took on a life of its own. It was an infinitely hungry organism, and in the end I saw that there was nothing to prevent it from becoming as large as the world itself. A life touches one life, which in turn touches another life, and very quickly the links are innumerable, beyond calculation. I knew about a fat woman in a small Louisiana town; I knew about a demented racist with tattoos on his fingers and a name that defied understanding. I knew about dozens of people I had never heard of before, and each one had been a part of Fanshawe's life. All well and good, perhaps, and one might say that this surplus of knowledge was the very thing that proved I was getting somewhere. I was a detective, after all, and my job was to hunt for clues. Faced with a million bits of random information, led down a million paths of false inquiry, I had to find the one path that would take me where I wanted to go. So far, the essential fact was that I hadn't found it. None of these people had seen or heard from Fanshawe in years, and short of doubting everything they told me, short of beginning an investigation into each one of them, I had to assume they were telling the truth.

What it boiled down to, I think, was a question of method. In some sense, I already knew everything there was to know about Fanshawe. The things I learned did not teach me anything important, did not go against any of the things I already knew. Or, to put it another way: the Fanshawe I had known was not the same Fanshawe I was looking for. There had been a break somewhere, a sudden, incomprehensible break—and the things I was told by the various people I questioned did not account for it. In the end, their statements only confirmed that what happened could not possibly have happened. That Fanshawe was kind, that Fanshawe was cruel—this was an old story, and I already knew it by heart. What I was looking for was something different, something I could not even imagine: a purely irrational act, a thing totally out of character, a contradiction of everything Fanshawe had been up to the moment he vanished. I kept trying to leap into the unknown, but each time I landed, I found myself on home ground, surrounded by what was most familiar to me.

The farther I went, the more the possibilities narrowed. Perhaps that was a good thing, I don't know. If nothing else, I knew that each time I failed, there would be one less place to look. Months went by, more months than I would like to admit. In February and March I spent most of my time looking for Quinn, the private detective who had worked for Sophie. Strangely enough, I couldn't find a trace of him. It seemed that he was no longer in business— not in New York, not anywhere. For a while I investigated reports of unclaimed bodies, questioned people who worked at the city morgue, tried to track down his family—but nothing came of it. As a last resort, I considered hiring another private detective to look for him, but then decided not to. One missing man was enough, I felt, and then, little by little, I used up the possibilities that were left. By mid-April, I was down to the last one. I held out for a few more days, hoping I would get lucky, but nothing developed. On the morning of the twenty-first, I finally walked into a travel agency and booked a flight to Paris.

I was supposed to leave on a Friday. On Tuesday, Sophie and I went shopping for a record player. One of her younger sisters was about to move to New York, and we were planning to give her our old record player as a present. The idea of replacing it had been in the air for several months, and this finally gave us an excuse to go looking for a new one. So we went downtown that Tuesday, bought the thing, and then lugged it home in a cab. We hooked it up in the same spot where the old one had been and then packed away the old one in the new box. A clever solution, we thought. Karen was due to arrive in May, and in the meantime we wanted to keep it somewhere out of sight. That was when we ran into a problem.

Storage space was limited, as it is in most New York apartments, and it seemed that we didn't have any left. The one closet that offered any hope was in the bedroom, but the floor was already crammed with boxes—three deep, two high, four across—and there wasn't enough room on the shelf above. These were the cartons that held Fanshawe's things (clothes, books, odds and ends), and they had been there since the day we moved in. Neither Sophie nor I had known what to do with them when she cleaned out her old place. We didn't want to be surrounded by memories of Fanshawe in our new life, but at the same time it seemed wrong just to throw the things away. The boxes had been a compromise, and eventually we no longer seemed to notice them. They became a part of the domestic landscape—like the broken floorboard under the living room rug, like the crack in the wall above our bed—invisible in the flux of daily life. Now, as Sophie opened the door of the closet and looked inside, her mood suddenly changed.

"Enough of this," she said, squatting down in the closet. She pushed away the clothes that were draped over the boxes, clicking hangers against each other, parting the jumble in frustration. It was an abrupt anger, and it seemed to be directed more at herself than at me.

"Enough of what?" I was standing on the other side of the bed, watching her back.

"All of it," she said, still flinging the clothes back and forth. "Enough of Fanshawe and his boxes."

"What do you want to do with them?" I sat down on the bed and waited for an answer, but she didn't say anything. "What do you want to do with them, Sophie?" I asked again.

She turned around and faced me, and I could see that she was on the point of tears. "What good is a closet if you can't even use it?" she said. Her voice was trembling, losing control. "I mean he's dead, isn't he? And if he's dead, why do we need all this . . . all this"—gesturing, groping for the word—"garbage. It's like living with a corpse."

"If you want, we can call the Salvation Army today," I said.

"Call them now. Before we say another word."

"I will. But first we'll have to open the boxes and sort through them."

"No. I want it to be everything, all at once."

"It's fine for the clothes," I said. "But I wanted to hold on to the books for a while. I've been meaning to make a list, and I wanted to check for any notes in the margins. I could finish in half an hour."

Sophie looked at me in disbelief. "You don't understand anything, do you?" she said. And then, as she stood up, the tears finally came out of her eyes—child's tears, tears that held nothing back, falling down her cheeks as if she didn't know they were there. "I can't get through to you anymore. You just don't hear what I'm saying."

"I'm doing my best, Sophie."

"No, you're not. You think you are, but you're not. Don't you see what's happening? You're bringing him back to life."

"I'm writing a book. That's all—just a book. But if I don't take it seriously, how can I hope to get it done?"

"There's more to it than that. I know it, I can feel it. If the two of us are going to last, he's got to be dead. Don't you understand that? Even if he's alive, he's got to be dead."

"What are you talking about? Of course he's dead."

"Not for much longer. Not if you keep it up."

"But you were the one who got me started. You wanted me to do the book."

"That was a hundred years ago, my darling. I'm so afraid I'm going to lose you. I couldn't take it if that happened."

"It's almost finished, I promise. This trip is the last step."

"And then what?"

"We'll see. I can't know what I'm getting into until I'm in it."

"That's what I'm afraid of."

"You could go with me."

"To Paris?"

"To Paris. The three of us could go together."

"I don't think so. Not the way things are now. You go alone. At least then, if you come back, it will be because you want to."

"What do you mean 'if'?"

"Just that. 'If.' As in, 'if you come back.'"

"You can't believe that."

"But I do. If things go on like this, I'm going to lose you."

"Don't talk like that, Sophie."

"I can't help it. You're so close to being gone already. I sometimes think I can see you vanishing before my eyes."

"That's nonsense."

"You're wrong. We're coming to the end, my darling, and you don't even know it. You're going to vanish, and I'll never see you again."

8

Things felt oddly bigger to me in Paris. The sky was more present than in New York, its whims more fragile. I found myself drawn to it, and for the first day or two I watched it constantly—sitting in my hotel room and studying the clouds, waiting for something to happen. These were northern clouds, the dream clouds that are always changing, massing up into huge gray mountains, discharging brief showers, dissipating, gathering again, rolling across the sun, refracting the light in ways that always seem different. The Paris sky has its own laws, and they function independently of the city below. If the buildings appear solid, anchored in the earth, indestructible, the sky is vast and amorphous, subject to constant turmoil. For the first week, I felt as though I had been turned upside-down. This was an old world city, and it had nothing to do with New York—with its slow skies and chaotic streets, its bland clouds and aggressive buildings. I had been displaced, and it made me suddenly unsure of myself. I felt my grip loosening, and at least once an hour I had to remind myself why I was there.

My French was neither good nor bad. I had enough to understand what people said to me, but speaking was difficult, and there were times when no words came to my lips, when I struggled to say even the simplest things. There was a certain pleasure in this, I believe—to experience language as a collection of sounds, to be forced to the surface of words where meanings vanish—but it was also quite wearing, and it had the effect of shutting me up in my thoughts. In order to understand what people were saying, I had to translate everything silently into English, which meant that even when I understood, I was understanding at one remove—doing twice the work and getting half the result. Nuances, subliminal associations, undercurrents—all these things were lost on me. In the end, it would probably not be wrong to say that everything was lost on me.

Still, I pushed ahead. It took me a few days to get the investigation started, but once I made my first contact, others followed. There were a number of disappointments, however. Wyshnegradsky was dead; I was unable to locate any of the people Fanshawe had tutored in English; the woman who had hired Fanshawe at the *New York Times* was gone, had not worked there in years. Such things were to be expected, but I took them hard, knowing that even the smallest gap could be fatal. These were empty spaces for me, blanks in the picture, and no matter how successful I was in filling the other areas, doubts would remain, which meant that the work could never be truly finished.

I spoke to the Dedmons, I spoke to the art book publishers Fanshawe had worked for, I spoke to the woman named Anne (a girlfriend, it turned out), I spoke to the movie producer. "Odd jobs," he said to me, in Russian-accented English, "that's what he did. Translations, script summaries, a little ghost writing for my wife. He was a smart boy, but too stiff. Very literary, if you know what I'm saying. I wanted to give him a chance to act—even offered to give him fencing and riding lessons for a picture we were going to do. I liked his looks, thought we could make something of him. But he wasn't interested. I've got other eggs to fry, he said. Something like that. It didn't matter. The picture made millions, and what do I care if the boy wants to act or not?"

There was something to be pursued here, but as I sat with this man in his monumental apartment on the Avenue Henri Martin, waiting for each sentence of his story between phone calls, I suddenly realized that I didn't need to hear any more. There was only one question that mattered, and this man couldn't answer it for me. If I stayed and listened to him, I would be given more details, more irrelevancies, yet another pile of useless notes. I had been pretending to write a book for too long now, and little by little I had forgotten my purpose. Enough, I said to myself, consciously echoing Sophie, enough of this, and then I stood up and left.

The point was that no one was watching me anymore. I no

longer had to put up a front as I had at home, no longer had to delude Sophie by creating endless busy-work for myself. The charade was over. I could discard my nonexistent book at last. For about ten minutes, walking back to my hotel across the river, I felt happier than I had in months. Things had been simplified, reduced to the clarity of a single problem. But then, the moment I absorbed this thought, I understood how bad the situation really was. I was coming to the end now, and I still hadn't found him. The mistake I was looking for had never surfaced. There were no leads, no clues, no tracks to follow. Fanshawe was buried some-where, and his whole life was buried with him. Unless he wanted to be found, I didn't have a ghost of a chance.

Still, I pushed ahead, trying to come to the end, to the very end, burrowing blindly through the last interviews, not willing to give up until I had seen everyone. I wanted to call Sophie. One day, I even went so far as to walk to the post office and wait in line for the foreign operator, but I didn't go through with it. Words were failing me constantly now, and I panicked at the thought of losing my nerve on the phone. What was I supposed to say, after all? Instead, I sent her a postcard with a photograph of Laurel and Hardy on it. On the back I wrote: "True marriages never make sense. Look at the couple on the other side. Proof that anything is possible, no? Perhaps we should start wearing derbies. At the very least, remember to clean out the closet before I return. Hugs to Ben."

I saw Anne Michaux the following afternoon, and she gave a little start when I entered the café where we had arranged to meet (Le Rouquet, Boulevárd Saint Germain). What she told me about Fanshawe is not important: who kissed who, what happened where, who said what, and so on. It comes down to more of the same. What I will mention, however, is that her initial double take was caused by the fact that she mistook me for Fanshawe. Just the briefest flicker, as she put it, and then it was gone. The resemblance had been noticed before, of course, but never so viscerally, with such immediate impact. I must have shown my reaction, for she quickly apologized (as if she had done something wrong) and returned to the point several times during the two or three hours we spent together—once even going out of her way to contradict herself: "I don't know what I was thinking. You don't look at all like him. It must have been the American in both of you."

Nevertheless, I found it disturbing, could not help feeling appalled. Something monstrous was happening, and I had no control over it anymore. The sky was growing dark inside—that much was certain; the ground was trembling. I found it hard to sit still, and I found it hard to move. From one moment to the next, I seemed to be in a different place, to forget where I was. Thoughts stop where the world begins, I kept telling myself. But the self is also in the world, I answered, and likewise the thoughts that come from it. The problem was that I could no longer make the right distinctions. This can never be that. Apples are not oranges, peaches are not plums. You feel the difference on your tongue, and then you know, as if inside yourself. But everything was beginning to have the same taste to me. I no longer felt hungry, I could no longer bring myself to eat.

As for the Dedmons, there is perhaps even less to say. Fanshawe could not have chosen more fitting benefactors, and of all the people I saw in Paris, they were the kindest, the most gracious. Invited to their apartment for drinks, I stayed on for dinner, and then, by the time we reached the second course, they were urging me to visit their house in the Var—the same house where Fanshawe had lived, and it needn't be a short visit, they said, since they were not planning to go there themselves until August. It had been an important place for Fanshawe and his work, Mr. Dedmon said, and no doubt my book would be enhanced if I saw it myself. I couldn't disagree with him, and no sooner were these words out of my mouth than Mrs. Dedmon was on the phone making arrangements for me in her precise and elegant French.

There was nothing to hold me in Paris anymore, and so I took the train the following afternoon. This was the end of the line for me, my southward trek to oblivion. Whatever hope I might have had (the faint possibility that Fanshawe had returned to France, the illogical thought that he had found refuge in the same place twice) evaporated by the time I got there. The house was empty; there was no sign of anyone. On the second day, examining the rooms on the upper floor, I came across a short poem Fanshawe had written on the wall—but I knew that poem already, and under it there was a date: August 25, 1972. He had never come back. I felt foolish now even for thinking it.

For want of anything better to do, I spent several days talking to people in the area: the nearby farmers, the villagers, the people of surrounding towns. I introduced myself by showing them a photograph of Fanshawe, pretending to be his brother, but feeling more like a down-and-out private eye, a buffoon clutching at straws. Some people remembered him, others didn't, still others weren't sure. It made no difference. I found the southern accent impenetrable (with its rolling r's and nasalized endings) and barely understood a word that was said to me. Of all the people I saw, only one had heard from Fanshawe since his departure. This was his closest neighbor—a tenant farmer who lived about a mile down the road. He was a peculiar little man of about forty, dirtier than anyone I had ever met. His house was a dank, crumbling seventeenth-century structure, and he seemed to live there by himself, with no companions but his truffle dog and hunting rifle. He was clearly proud of having been Fanshawe's friend, and to prove how close they had been he showed me a white cowboy hat that Fanshawe had sent to him after returning to America. There was no reason not to believe his story. The hat was still in its original box and apparently had never been worn. He explained that he was saving it for the right moment, and then launched into a political harangue that I had trouble following. The revolution was coming, he said, and when it did, he was going to buy a white horse and a machine gun, put on his hat, and ride down the main street in town, plugging all the shopkeepers who had collaborated with the Germans during the War. Just like in America, he added. When I asked him what he meant, he delivered a rambling, hallucinatory lecture about cowboys and Indians. But that was a long time ago, I said, trying to cut him short. No, no, he insisted, it still goes on today. Didn't I know about the shootouts on Fifth Avenue? Hadn't I heard of the Apaches? It was pointless to argue. In defense of my ignorance, I told him that I lived in another neighborhood.

I stayed on in the house for a few more days. My plan was to do nothing for as long as I could, to rest up. I was exhausted, and I needed a chance to regroup before going back to Paris. A day or two went by. I walked through the fields, visited the woods, sat out in the sun reading French translations of American detective novels. It should have been the perfect cure: holing up in the middle of nowhere, letting my mind float free. But none of it really helped. The house wouldn't make room for me, and by the third day I sensed that I was no longer alone, that I could never be alone in that place. Fanshawe was there, and no matter how hard I tried not to think about him, I couldn't escape. This was unexpected, galling. Now that I had stopped looking for him, he was more present to me than ever before. The whole process had been reversed. After all these months of trying to find him, I felt as though I was the one who had been found. Instead of looking for Fanshawe, I had actually been running away from him. The work I had contrived for myself—the false book, the endless detours—had been no more than an attempt to ward him off, a ruse to keep him as far away from me as possible. For if I could convince myself that I was looking for him, then it necessarily followed that he was somewhere else—somewhere beyond me, beyond the limits of my life. But I had been wrong. Fanshawe was exactly where I was, and he had been there since the beginning. From the moment his letter arrived, I had been struggling to imagine him, to see him as he might have been—but my mind had always conjured a blank. At best, there was one impoverished image: the door of a locked room. That was the extent of it: Fanshawe alone in that room, condemned to a mythical solitude—living perhaps, breathing perhaps, dreaming God knows what. This room, I now discovered, was located inside my skull.

Strange things happened to me after that. I returned to Paris, but once there I found myself with nothing to do. I didn't want to look up any of the people I had seen before, and I didn't have the courage to go back to New York. I became inert, a thing that could not move, and little by little I lost track of myself. If I am able to say anything about this period at all, it is only because I have certain documentary evidence to help me. The visa stamps in my passport, for example; my airplane ticket, my hotel bill, and so on. These things prove to me that I remained in Paris for more than a month. But that is very different from remembering, and in spite of what I know, I still find it impossible. I see things that happened, I encounter images of myself in various places, but only at a distance, as though I were watching someone else. None of it feels like memory, which is always anchored within; it's out there beyond what I can feel or touch, beyond anything that has to do with me. I have lost a month from my life, and even now it is a difficult thing for me to confess, a thing that fills me with shame.

A month is a long time, more than enough time for a man to come apart. Those days come back to me in fragments when they come at all, bits and pieces that refuse to add up. I see myself falling down drunk on the street one night, standing up, staggering towards a lamppost, and then vomiting all over my shoes. I see myself sitting in a movie theater with the lights on and watching a crowd of people file out around me, unable to remember the film I had just seen. I see myself prowling the rue Saint-Denis at night, picking out prostitutes to sleep with, my head burning with the thought of bodies, an endless jumble of naked breasts, naked thighs, naked buttocks. I see my cock being sucked,

I see myself on a bed with two girls kissing each other, I see an enormous black woman spreading her legs on a bidet and washing her cunt. I will not try to say that these things are not real, that they did not happen. It's just that I can't account for them. I was fucking the brains out of my head, drinking myself into another world. But if the point was to obliterate Fanshawe, then my binge was a success. He was gone—and I was gone along with him.

The end, however, is clear to me. I have not forgotten it, and I feel lucky to have kept that much. The entire story comes down to what happened at the end, and without that end inside me now, I could not have started this book. The same holds for the two books that come before it, *City of Glass* and *Ghosts*. These three stories are finally the same story, but each one represents a different stage in my awareness of what it is about. I don't claim to have solved any problems. I am merely suggesting that a moment came when it no longer frightened me to look at what had happened. If words followed, it was only because I had no choice but to accept them, to take them upon myself and go where they wanted me to go. But that does not necessarily make the words important. I have been struggling to say goodbye to something for a long time now, and this struggle is all that really matters. The story is not in the words; it's in the struggle.

One night, I found myself in a bar near the Place Pigalle. *Found* is the term I wish to use, for I have no idea of how

I got there, no memory of entering the place at all. It was one of those clip joints that are common in the neighborhood: six or eight girls at the bar, the chance to sit at a table with one of them and buy an exorbitantly priced bottle of champagne, and then, if one is so inclined, the possibility of coming to a certain financial agreement and retiring to the privacy of a room in the hotel next door. The scene begins for me as I'm sitting at one of the tables with a girl, just having received the bucket of champagne. The girl was Tahitian, I remember, and she was beautiful: no more than nineteen or twenty, very small, and wearing a dress of white netting with nothing underneath, a crisscross of cables over her smooth brown skin. The effect was superbly erotic. I remember her round breasts visible in the diamond-shaped openings, the overwhelming softness of her neck when I leaned over and kissed it. She told me her name, but I insisted on calling her Fayaway, telling her that she was an exile from Typee and that I was Herman Melville, an American sailor who had come all the way from New York to rescue her. She hadn't the vaguest idea of what I was talking about, but she continued to smile, no doubt thinking me crazy as I rambled on in my sputtering French, unperturbed, laughing when I laughed, allowing me to kiss her wherever I liked.

We were sitting in an alcove in the corner, and from my seat I was able to take in the rest of the room. Men came and went, some popping their heads through the door and leaving, some staying for a drink at the bar, one or two going to a table as I had done. After about fifteen minutes, a young man came in who was obviously American. He seemed nervous to me, as if he had never been in such a place before, but his French was surprisingly good, and as he fluently ordered a whiskey at the bar and started talking to one of the girls, I saw that he meant to stay for a while. I studied him from my little nook, continuing to run my hand along Fayaway's leg and to nuzzle her with my face, but the longer he stood there, the more distracted I became. He was tall, athletically built, with sandy hair and an open, somewhat boyish manner. I guessed his age at twenty-six or twenty-seven—a graduate student, perhaps, or else a young lawyer working for an American firm in Paris. I had never seen this man before, and yet there was something familiar about him, something that stopped me from turning away: a brief scald, a weird synapse of recognition. I tried out various names on him, shunted him through the past, unravelled the spool of associations—but nothing happened. He's no one, I said to myself, finally giving up. And then, out of the blue, by some muddled chain of reasoning, I finished the thought by adding: and if he's no one, then he must be Fanshawe. I laughed out loud at my joke. Ever on the alert, Fayaway laughed with me. I knew that nothing could be more absurd, but I said it again: Fanshawe. And then again: Fanshawe. And the more I said it, the more it pleased me to say it. Each time the word came out of my

mouth, another burst of laughter followed. I was intoxi-
cated by the sound of it; it drove me to a pitch of
raucousness, and little by little Fayaway seemed to grow
confused. She had probably thought I was referring to some
sexual practice, making some joke she couldn't understand,
but my repetitions had gradually robbed the word of its
meaning, and she began to hear it as a threat. I looked at
the man across the room and spoke the word again. My
happiness was immeasurable. I exulted in the sheer falsity
of my assertion, celebrating the new power I had just
bestowed upon myself. I was the sublime alchemist who
could change the world at will. This man was Fanshawe
because I said he was Fanshawe, and that was all there was
to it. Nothing could stop me anymore. Without even
pausing to think, I whispered into Fayaway's ear that I
would be right back, disengaged myself from her wonderful
arms, and sauntered over to the pseudo-Fanshawe at the
bar. In my best imitation of an Oxford accent, I said:

"Well, old man, fancy that. We meet again."

He turned around and looked at me carefully. The smile
that had been forming on his face slowly diminished into a
frown. "Do I know you?" he finally asked.

"Of course you do," I said, all bluster and good humor.
"The name's Melville. Herman Melville. Perhaps you've
read some of my books."

He didn't know whether to treat me as a jovial drunk or
a dangerous psychopath, and the confusion showed on his

face. It was a splendid confusion, and I enjoyed it thoroughly.

"Well," he said at last, forcing out a little smile, "I might have read one or two."

"The one about the whale, no doubt."

"Yes. The one about the whale."

"I'm glad to hear it," I said, nodding pleasantly, and then put my arm around his shoulder. "And so, Fanshawe," I said, "what brings you to Paris this time of year?"

The confusion returned to his face. "Sorry," he said, "I didn't catch that name."

"Fanshawe."

"Fanshawe?"

"Fanshawe. F-A-N-S-H-A-W-E."

"Well," he said, relaxing into a broad grin, suddenly sure of himself again, "that's the problem right there. You've mixed me up with someone else. My name isn't Fanshawe. It's Stillman. Peter Stillman."

"No problem," I answered, giving him a little squeeze. "If you want to call yourself Stillman, that's fine with me. Names aren't important, after all. What matters is that I know who you really are. You're Fanshawe. I knew it the moment you walked in. 'There's the old devil himself,' I said. 'I wonder what he's doing in a place like this?' "

He was beginning to lose patience with me now. He removed my arm from his shoulder and backed off. "That's enough," he said. "You've made a mistake, and let's leave it at that. I don't want to talk to you anymore."

"Too late," I said. "Your secret's out, my friend. There's no way to hide from me now."

"Leave me alone," he said, showing anger for the first time. "I don't talk to lunatics. Leave me alone, or there'll be trouble."

The other people in the bar couldn't understand what we were saying, but the tension had become obvious, and I could feel myself being watched, could feel the mood shift around me. Stillman suddenly seemed to panic. He shot a glance at the woman behind the bar, looked apprehensively at the girl beside him, and then made an impulsive decision to leave. He pushed me out of his way and started for the door. I could have let it go at that, but I didn't. I was just getting warmed up, and I didn't want my inspiration to be wasted. I went back to where Fayaway was sitting and put a few hundred francs on the table. She feigned a pout in response. "C'est mon frère," I said. "Il est fou. Je dois le poursuivre." And then, as she reached for the money, I blew her a kiss, turned around, and left.

Stillman was twenty or thirty yards ahead of me, walking quickly down the street. I kept pace with him, hanging back to avoid being noticed, but not letting him move out of sight. Every now and then he looked back over his shoulder, as though expecting me to be there, but I don't think he saw me until we were well out of the neighborhood, away from the crowds and commotion, slicing through the quiet, darkened core of the Right Bank. The encounter had spooked him, and he behaved like a man running for his life. But that was not difficult to understand. I was the thing we all fear most: the belligerent stranger who steps out from the shadows, the knife that stabs us in the back, the speeding car that crushes us to death. He was right to be running, but his fear only egged me on, goaded me to pursue him, made me rabid with determination. I had no plan, no idea of what I was going to do, but I followed him without the slightest doubt, knowing that my whole life hinged on it. It is important to stress that by now I was completely lucid—no wobbling, no drunkenness, utterly clear in my head. I realized that I was acting outrageously. Stillman was not Fanshawe—I knew that. He was an arbitrary choice, totally innocent and blank. But that was the thing that thrilled me—the randomness of it, the vertigo of pure chance. It made no sense, and because of that, it made all the sense in the world.

A moment came when the only sounds in the street were our footsteps. Stillman looked back again and finally saw me. He began moving faster, breaking into a trot. I called after him: "Fanshawe." I called after him again: "It's too late. I know who you are, Fanshawe." And then, on the next street: "It's all over, Fanshawe. You'll never get away." Stillman said nothing in response, did not even bother to turn around. I wanted to keep talking to him, but by now he was running, and if I tried to talk, it would only have slowed me down. I abandoned my taunts and went after him. I have no idea how long we ran, but it seemed to go on for hours. He was younger than I was, younger and stronger, and I almost lost him, almost didn't make it. I pushed myself down the dark street, passing the point of exhaustion, of sickness, frantically hurtling toward him, not allowing myself to stop. Long before I reached him, long before I even knew I was going to reach him, I felt as though I was no longer inside myself. I can think of no other way to express it. I couldn't feel myself anymore. The sensation of life had dribbled out of me, and in its place there was a miraculous euphoria, a sweet poison rushing through my blood, the undeniable odor of nothingness. This is the moment of my death, I said to myself, this is when I die. A second later, I caught up to Stillman and tackled him from behind. We went crashing to the pavement, the two of us grunting on impact. I had used up all my strength, and by now I was too short of breath to defend myself, too drained to struggle. Not a word was said. For several seconds we grappled on the sidewalk, but then he managed to break free of my grip, and after that there was nothing I could do. He started pounding me with his fists, kicking me with the points of his shoes, pummelling me all over. I remember trying to protect my face with my hands; I remember the pain and how it stunned me, how much it hurt and how desperately I wanted not to feel it anymore. But it couldn't have lasted very long, for nothing else comes back to me. Stillman tore me apart, and by the time he was finished, I was out cold. I can remember waking up on the sidewalk and being surprised that it was still night, but that's the extent of it. Everything else is gone.

For the next three days I didn't move from my hotel room. The shock was not so much that I was in pain, but that it would not be strong enough to kill me. I realized this by the second or third day. At a certain moment, lying there on the bed and looking at the slats of the closed shutters, I understood that I had lived through it. It felt strange to be alive, almost incomprehensible. One of my fingers was broken; both temples were gashed; it ached even to breathe. But that was somehow beside the point. I was alive, and the more I thought about it, the less I understood. It did not seem possible that I had been spared.

Later that same night, I wired Sophie that I was coming home.

9

I am nearly at the end now. There is one thing left, but that did not happen until later, until three more years had passed. In the meantime, there were many difficulties, many dramas, but I do not think they belong to the story I am trying to tell. After my return to New York, Sophie and I lived apart for almost a year. She had given up on me, and there were months of confusion before I finally won her back. From the vantage point of this moment (May 1984), that is the only thing that matters. Beside it, the facts of my life are purely incidental.

On February 23, 1981, Ben's baby brother was born. We named him Paul, in memory of Sophie's grandfather. Several months later (in July) we moved across the river, renting the top two floors of a brownstone house in Brooklyn. In September, Ben started kindergarten. We all went to Minnesota for Christmas, and by the time we got back, Paul was walking on his own. Ben, who had gradually taken him under his wing, claimed full credit for the development.

As for Fanshawe, Sophie and I never talked about him.

This was our silent pact, and the longer we said nothing, the more we proved our loyalty to each other. After I returned the advance money to Stuart Green and officially stopped writing the biography, we mentioned him only once. That came on the day we decided to live together again, and it was couched in strictly practical terms. Fanshawe's books and plays had continued to produce a good income. If we were going to stay married, Sophie said, then using the money for ourselves was out of the question. I agreed with her. We found other ways to earn what we had to and placed the royalty money in trust for Ben—and subsequently for Paul as well. As a final step, we hired a literary agent to manage the business of Fanshawe's work: requests to perform plays, reprint negotiations, contracts, whatever needed to be done. To the extent that we were able to act, we did. If Fanshawe still had the power to destroy us, it would only be because we wanted him to, because we wanted to destroy ourselves. That was why I never bothered to tell Sophie the truth—not because it frightened me, but because the truth was no longer important. Our strength was in our silence, and I had no intention of breaking it.

Still, I knew that the story wasn't over. My last month in Paris had taught me that, and little by little I learned to accept it. It was only a matter of time before the next thing happened. This seemed inevitable to me, and rather than deny it anymore, rather than delude myself with the thought that I could ever get rid of Fanshawe, I tried to prepare myself for it, tried to make myself ready for anything. It is the power of this *anything*, I believe, that has made the story so difficult to tell. For when anything can happen—that is the precise moment when words begin to fail. To the degree that Fanshawe became inevitable, that was the degree to which he was no longer there. I learned to accept this. I learned to live with him in the same way I lived with the thought of my own death. Fanshawe himself was not death—but he was like death, and he functioned as a trope for death inside me. If not for my breakdown in Paris, I never would have understood this. I did not die there, but I came close, and there was a moment, perhaps there were several moments, when I tasted death, when I saw myself dead. There is no cure for such an encounter. Once it happens, it goes on happening; you live with it for the rest of your life.

The letter came early in the spring of 1982. This time the postmark was from Boston, and the message was terse, more urgent than before. "Impossible to hold out any longer," it said. "Must talk to you. 9 Columbus Square, Boston; April 1st. This is where it ends, I promise."

I had less than a week to invent an excuse for going to Boston. This turned out to be more difficult than it should have been. Although I persisted in not wanting Sophie to know anything (feeling that it was the least I could do for her), I somehow balked at telling another lie, even though it had to be done. Two or three days slipped by without any progress, and in the end I concocted some lame story about having to consult papers in the Harvard Library. I can't even remember what papers they were supposed to be. Something to do with an article I was going to write, I think, but that could be wrong. The important thing was that Sophie did not raise any objections. Fine, she said, go right ahead, and so on. My gut feeling is that she suspected something was up, but that is only a feeling, and it would be pointless to speculate about it here. Where Sophie is concerned, I tend to believe that nothing is hidden.

I booked a seat for April first on the early train. On the morning of my departure, Paul woke up a little before five and climbed into bed with us. I roused myself an hour later and crept out of the room, pausing briefly at the door to watch Sophie and the baby in the dim gray light—sprawled out, impervious, the bodies I belonged to. Ben was in the kitchen upstairs, already dressed, eating a banana and drawing pictures. I scrambled some eggs for the two of us and told him that I was about to take a train to Boston. He wanted to know where Boston was.

"About two hundred miles from here," I said.

"Is that as far away as space?"

"If you went straight up, you'd be getting close."

"I think you should go to the moon. A rocket ship is better than a train."

"I'll do that on the way back. They have regular flights

from Boston to the moon on Fridays. I'll reserve a seat the moment I get there."

"Good. Then you can tell me what it's like."

"If I find a moon rock, I'll bring one back for you."

"What about Paul?"

"I'll get one for him, too."

"No thanks."

"What does that mean?"

"I don't want a moon rock. Paul would put his in his mouth and choke."

"What would you like instead?"

"An elephant."

"There aren't any elephants in space."

"I know that. But you aren't going to space."

"True."

"And I bet there are elephants in Boston."

"You're probably right. Do you want a pink elephant or a white elephant?"

"A gray elephant. A big fat one with lots of wrinkles."

"No problem. Those are the easiest ones to find. Would you like it wrapped up in a box, or should I bring it home on a leash?"

"I think you should ride it home. Sitting on top with a crown on your head. Just like an emperor."

"The emperor of what?"

"The emperor of little boys."

"Do I get to have an empress?"

"Of course. Mommy is the empress. She'd like that. Maybe we should wake her up and tell her."

"Let's not. I'd rather surprise her with it when I get home."

"Good idea. She won't believe it until she sees it anyway."

"Exactly. And we don't want her to be disappointed. In case I can't find the elephant."

"Oh, you'll find it, Dad. Don't worry about that."

"How can you be so sure?"

"Because you're the emperor. An emperor can get anything he wants."

It rained the whole way up, the sky even threatening snow by the time we reached Providence. In Boston, I bought myself an umbrella and covered the last two or three miles on foot. The streets were gloomy in the piss-gray air, and as I walked to the South End, I saw almost no one: a drunk, a group of teenagers, a telephone man, two or three stray mutts. Columbus Square consisted of ten or twelve houses in a row, fronting on a cobbled island that cut it off from the main thoroughfare. Number nine was the most dilapidated of the lot—four stories like the others, but sagging, with boards propping up the entranceway and the brick facade in need of mending. Still, there was an impressive solidity to it, a nineteenth-century elegance that continued to show through the cracks. I imagined large rooms with high ceilings, comfortable ledges by the bay window, molded ornaments in the plaster. But I did not get to see any of these things. As it turned out, I never got beyond the front hall.

There was a rusted metal clapper in the door, a half-sphere with a handle in the center, and when I twisted the handle, it made the sound of someone retching—a muffled, gagging sound that did not carry very far. I waited, but nothing happened. I twisted the bell again, but no one came. Then, testing the door with my hand, I saw that it wasn't locked—pushed it open, paused, and went in. The front hall was empty. To my right was the staircase, with its mahogany banister and bare wooden steps; to my left were closed double doors, blocking off what was no doubt the parlor; straight ahead there was another door, also closed, that probably led to the kitchen. I hesitated for a moment, decided on the stairs, and was about to go up when I heard something from behind the double doors—a faint tapping, followed by a voice I couldn't understand. I turned from the staircase and looked at the door, listening for the voice again. Nothing happened.

A long silence. Then, almost in a whisper, the voice spoke again. "In here," it said.

I went to the doors and pressed my ear against the crack between them. "Is that you, Fanshawe?"

"Don't use that name," the voice said, more distinctly

this time. "I won't allow you to use that name." The mouth of the person inside was lined up directly with my ear. Only the door was between us, and we were so close that I felt as if the words were being poured into my head. It was like listening to a man's heart beating in his chest, like searching a body for a pulse. He stopped talking, and I could feel his breath slithering through the crack.

"Let me in," I said. "Open the door and let me in."

"I can't do that," the voice answered. "We'll have to talk like this."

I grabbed hold of the door knob and shook the doors in frustration. "Open up," I said. "Open up, or I'll break the door down."

"No," said the voice. "The door stays closed." By now I was convinced that it was Fanshawe in there. I wanted it to be an imposter, but I recognized too much in that voice to pretend it was anyone else. "I'm standing here with a gun," he said, "and it's pointed right at you. If you come through the door, I'll shoot."

"I don't believe you."

"Listen to this," he said, and then I heard him turn away from the door. A second later a gun went off, followed by the sound of plaster falling to the floor. I tried to peer through the crack in the meantime, hoping to catch a glimpse of the room, but the space was too narrow. I could see no more than a thread of light, a single gray filament. Then the mouth returned, and I could no longer see even that.

"All right," I said, "you have a gun. But if you don't let me see you, how will I know you are who you say you are?"

"I haven't said who I am."

"Let me put it another way. How can I know I'm talking to the right person?"

"You'll have to trust me."

"At this late date, trust is about the last thing you should expect."

"I'm telling you that I'm the right person. That should be enough. You've come to the right place, and I'm the right person."

"I thought you wanted to see me. That's what you said in your letter."

"I said that I wanted to talk to you. There's a difference."

"Let's not split hairs."

"I'm just reminding you of what I wrote."

"Don't push me too far, Fanshawe. There's nothing to stop me from walking out."

I heard a sudden intake of breath, and then a hand slapped violently against the door. "Not Fanshawe!" he shouted. "Not Fanshawe—ever again!"

I let a few moments pass, not wanting to provoke another outburst. The mouth withdrew from the crack, and I imagined that I heard groans from somewhere in the middle of the room—groans or sobs, I couldn't tell which. I stood there waiting, not knowing what to say next. Eventually,

the mouth returned, and after another long pause
Fanshawe said, "Are you still there?"

"Yes."

"Forgive me. I didn't want it to begin like this."

"Just remember," I said, "I'm only here because you
asked me to come."

"I know that. And I'm grateful to you for it."

"It might help if you explained why you invited me."

"Later. I don't want to talk about that yet."

"Then what?"

"Other things. The things that have happened."

"I'm listening."

"Because I don't want you to hate me. Can you understand that?"

"I don't hate you. There was a time when I did, but I'm
over that now."

"Today is my last day, you see. And I had to make sure."

"Is this where you've been all along?"

"I came here about two years ago, I think."

"And before that?"

"Here and there. That man was after me, and I had to
keep moving. It gave me a feeling for travel, a real taste for
it. Not at all what I had expected. My plan had always been
to sit still and let the time run out."

"You're talking about Quinn?"

"Yes. The private detective."

"Did he find you?"

"Twice. Once in New York. The next time down South."

"Why did he lie about it?"

"Because I scared him to death. He knew what would happen to him if anyone found out."

"He disappeared, you know. I couldn't find a trace of him."

"He's somewhere. It's not important."

"How did you manage to get rid of him?"

"I turned everything around. He thought he was following me, but in fact I was following him. He found me in New York, of course, but I got away—wriggled right through his arms. After that, it was like playing a game. I led him along, leaving clues for him everywhere, making it impossible for him not to find me. But I was watching him the whole time, and when the moment came, I set him up, and he walked straight into my trap."

"Very clever."

"No. It was stupid. But I didn't have any choice. It was either that or get hauled back—which would have meant being treated like a crazy man. I hated myself for it. He was only doing his job, after all, and it made me feel sorry for him. Pity disgusts me, especially when I find it in myself."

"And then?"

"I couldn't be sure if my trick had really worked. I thought Quinn might come after me again. And so I kept on moving, even when I didn't have to. I lost about a year like that."

"Where did you go?"

"The South, the Southwest. I wanted to stay where it was warm. I travelled on foot, you see, slept outside, tried to go where there weren't many people. It's an enormous country, you know. Absolutely bewildering. At one point, I stayed in the desert for about two months. Later, I lived in a shack at the edge of a Hopi reservation in Arizona. The Indians had a tribal council before giving me permission to stay there."

"You're making this up."

"I'm not asking you to believe me. I'm telling you the story, that's all. You can think anything you want."

"And then?"

"I was somewhere in New Mexico. I went into a diner along the road one day to get a bite to eat, and someone had left a newspaper on the counter. So I picked it up and read it. That's when I found out that a book of mine had been published."

"Were you surprised?"

"That's not quite the word I would use."

"What, then?"

"I don't know. Angry, I think. Upset."

"I don't understand."

"I was angry because the book was garbage."

"Writers never know how to judge their work."

"No, the book was garbage, believe me. Everything I did was garbage."

"Then why didn't you destroy it?"

"I was too attached to it. But that doesn't make it good. A baby is attached to his caca, but no one fusses about it. It's strictly his own business."

"Then why did you make Sophie promise to show me the work?"

"To appease her. But you know that already. You figured that out a long time ago. That was my excuse. My real reason was to find a new husband for her."

"It worked."

"It had to work. I didn't pick just anyone, you know."

"And the manuscripts?"

"I thought you would throw them away. It never occurred to me that anyone would take the work seriously."

"What did you do after you read that the book had been published?"

"I went back to New York. It was an absurd thing to do, but I was a little beside myself, not thinking clearly anymore. The book trapped me into what I had done, you see, and I had to wrestle with it all over again. Once the book was published, I couldn't turn back."

"I thought you were dead."

"That's what you were supposed to think. If nothing else, it proved to me that Quinn was no longer a problem. But this new problem was much worse. That's when I wrote you the letter."

"That was a vicious thing to do."

"I was angry at you. I wanted you to suffer, to live with

the same things I had to live with. The instant after I
dropped it in the mailbox, I regretted it."

"Too late."

"Yes. Too late."

"How long did you stay in New York?"

"I don't know. Six or eight months, I think."

"How did you live? How did you earn the money to live?"

"I stole things."

"Why don't you tell the truth?"

"I'm doing my best. I'm telling you everything I'm able to
tell."

"What else did you do in New York?"

"I watched you. I watched you and Sophie and the baby.
There was even a time when I camped outside your
apartment building. For two or three weeks, maybe a
month. I followed you everywhere you went. Once or twice,
I even bumped into you on the street, looked you straight in
the eye. But you never noticed. It was fantastic the way you
didn't see me."

"You're making all this up."

"I must not look the same anymore."

"No one can change that much."

"I think I'm unrecognizable. But that was a lucky thing
for you. If anything had happened, I probably would have
killed you. That whole time in New York, I was filled with
murderous thoughts. Bad stuff. I came close to a kind of
horror there."

"What stopped you?"

"I found the courage to leave."

"That was noble of you."

"I'm not trying to defend myself. I'm just giving you the story."

"Then what?"

"I shipped out again. I still had my merchant seaman's card, and I signed on with a Greek freighter. It was disgusting, truly repulsive from beginning to end. But I deserved it; it was exactly what I wanted. The ship went everywhere—India, Japan, all over the world. I didn't get off once. Every time we came to a port, I would go down to my cabin and lock myself in. I spent two years like that, seeing nothing, doing nothing, living like a dead man."

"While I was trying to write the story of your life."

"Is that what you were doing?"

"So it would seem."

"A big mistake."

"You don't have to tell me. I found that out for myself."

"The ship pulled into Boston one day, and I decided to get off. I had saved a tremendous amount of money, more than enough to buy this house. I've been here ever since."

"What name have you been using?"

"Henry Dark. But no one knows who I am. I never go out. There's a woman who comes twice a week and brings me what I need, but I never see her. I leave her a note at the foot of the stairs, along with the money I owe her. It's a simple and effective arrangement. You're the first person I've spoken to in two years."

"Do you ever think that you're out of your mind?"

"I know it looks like that to you—but I'm not, believe me. I don't even want to waste my breath talking about it. What I need for myself is very different from what other people need."

"Isn't this house a bit big for one person?"

"Much too big. I haven't been above the ground floor since the day I moved in."

"Then why did you buy it?"

"It cost almost nothing. And I liked the name of the street. It appealed to me."

"Columbus Square?"

"Yes."

"I don't follow."

"It seemed like a good omen. Coming back to America—and then finding a house on a street named after Columbus. There was a certain logic to it."

"And this is where you're planning to die."

"Exactly."

"Your first letter said seven years. You still have a year to go."

"I've proved the point to myself. There's no need to go on with it. I'm tired. I've had enough."

"Did you ask me to come here because you thought I would stop you?"

"No. Not at all. I'm not expecting anything from you."

"Then what do you want?"

"I have some things to give you. At a certain point, I realized that I owed you an explanation for what I did. At least an attempt. I've spent the past six months trying to get it down on paper."

"I thought you gave up writing for good."

"This is different. It has no connection with what I used to do."

"Where is it?"

"Behind you. On the floor of the closet under the stairs. A red notebook."

I turned around, opened the closet door, and picked up the notebook. It was a standard spiral affair with two hundred ruled pages. I gave a quick glance at the contents and saw that all the pages had been filled: the same familiar writing, the same black ink, the same small letters. I stood up and returned to the crack between the doors.

"What now?" I asked.

"Take it home with you. Read it."

"What if I can't?"

"Then save it for the boy. He might want to see it when he grows up."

"I don't think you have any right to ask that."

"He's my son."

"No, he's not. He's mine."

"I won't insist. Read it yourself, then. It was written for you anyway."

"And Sophie?"

"No. You mustn't tell her."

"That's the one thing I'll never understand."

"Sophie?"

"How you could walk out on her like that. What did she ever do to you?"

"Nothing. It wasn't her fault. You must know that by now. It's just that I wasn't meant to live like other people."

"How were you meant to live?"

"It's all in the notebook. Whatever I managed to say now would only distort the truth."

"Is there anything else?"

"No, I don't think so. We've probably come to the end."

"I don't believe you have the nerve to shoot me. If I broke down the door now, you wouldn't do a thing."

"Don't risk it. You'd die for nothing."

"I'd pull the gun out of your hand. I'd knock you senseless."

"There's no point to that. I'm already dead. I took poison hours ago."

"I don't believe you."

"You can't possibly know what's true or not true. You'll never know."

"I'll call the police. They'll chop down the door and drag you off to the hospital."

"One sound at the door—and a bullet goes through my head. There's no way you can win."

"Is death so tempting?"

"I've lived with it for so long now, it's the only thing I have left."

I no longer knew what to say. Fanshawe had used me up, and as I heard him breathing on the other side of the door, I felt as if the life were being sucked out of me. "You're a fool," I said, unable to think of anything else. "You're a fool, and you deserve to die." Then, overwhelmed by my own weakness and stupidity, I started pounding the door like a child, shaking and sputtering, on the point of tears.

"You'd better go now," Fanshawe said. "There's no reason to drag this out."

"I don't want to go," I said. "We still have things to talk about."

"No, we don't. It's finished. Take the notebook and go back to New York. That's all I ask of you."

I was so exhausted that for a moment I thought I was going to fall down. I clung to the doorknob for support, my head going black inside, struggling not to pass out. After that, I have no memory of what happened. I found myself outside, in front of the house, the umbrella in one hand and the red notebook in the other. The rain had stopped, but the air was still raw, and I could feel the dankness in my lungs. I watched a large truck clatter by in the traffic, following its red taillight until I couldn't see it anymore. When I looked up, I saw that it was almost night. I started walking away from the house, mechanically putting one foot in front of the other, unable to concentrate on where I was going. I think I fell down once or twice. At one point, I remember waiting on a corner and trying to get a cab, but no one stopped for me. A few minutes after that, the umbrella slipped from my hand and fell into a puddle. I didn't bother to pick it up.

It was just after seven o'clock when I arrived at South Station. A train for New York had left fifteen minutes earlier, and the next one wasn't scheduled until eight-thirty. I sat down on one of the wooden benches with the red notebook on my lap. A few late commuters straggled in; a janitor slowly moved across the marble floor with a mop; I listened in as two men talked about the Red Sox behind me. After ten minutes of fighting off the impulse, I at last opened the notebook. I read steadily for almost an hour, flipping back and forth among the pages, trying to get a sense of what Fanshawe had written. If I say nothing about what I found there, it is because I understood very little. All the words were familiar to me, and yet they seemed to have been put together strangely, as though their final purpose was to cancel each other out. I can think of no other way to express it. Each sentence erased the sentence before it, each paragraph made the next paragraph impossible. It is odd, then, that the feeling that survives from this notebook is one of great lucidity. It is as if Fanshawe knew his final work had to subvert every expectation I had for it. These were not the words of a man who regretted anything. He had answered the question by asking another question, and therefore everything remained open, unfinished, to be started again. I lost my way after the first word, and from then on I could only grope ahead, faltering in the darkness, blinded by the book that had been written for me. And yet, underneath this confusion, I felt there was something too willed, something too perfect, as though in the end the only thing he had really wanted was to fail—even to the point of failing himself. I could be wrong, however. I was hardly in a condition to be reading anything at that moment, and my judgment is possibly askew. I was there, I read those words with my own eyes, and yet I find it hard to trust in what I am saying.

I wandered out to the tracks several minutes in advance. It was raining again, and I could see my breath in the air before me, leaving my mouth in little bursts of fog. One by one, I tore the pages from the notebook, crumpled them in my hand, and dropped them into a trash bin on the platform. I came to the last page just as the train was pulling out.